A Candlelight Ecstasy Romance

THE WORLD DISAPPEARED IN SWIRLS OF BLUE AND WHITE AND PURE BLINDING SILVER . . .

She was in his arms. His mouth was warm, stirring her senses in ways she'd only dreamed of before. He let his lips slide down her cheek to her ear while his arms pressed her close. She heard his quick, rough breath whisper past her ear, then his mouth was on hers once more. She tasted salt, felt the powerful muscles of his shoulders tense, felt the sea rock them both gently in its watery embrace, and felt her body dissolving against his like molten gold . . .

A CANDLELIGHT ECSTASY ROMANCE ®

WHITE SAND, WILD SEA

Diana Blayne

A CANDLELIGHT ECSTASY ROMANCE ®

Published by
Dell Publishing Co., Inc.
1 Dag Hammarskjold Plaza
New York, New York 10017

Dell ® TM 681510, Dell Publishing Co., Inc.

Candlelight Ecstasy Romance®, 1,203,540, is a registered
trademark of Dell Publishing Co., Inc.,
New York, New York.

ISBN: 0-440-19627-2

Printed in the United States of America
First printing—May 1983

*For Trudy, Helene, Shirley, Kay,
Cindy, Brenda, Antonia, and Nancy*

To Our Readers:

We have been delighted with your enthusiastic response to Candlelight Ecstasy Romances®, and we thank you for the interest you have shown in this exciting series.

In the upcoming months we will continue to present the distinctive, sensuous love stories you have come to expect only from Ecstasy. We look forward to bringing you many more books from your favorite authors and also the very finest work from new authors of contemporary romantic fiction.

As always we are striving to present the unique absorbing love stories that you enjoy most—books that are more than ordinary romance.

Your suggestions and comments are always welcome. Please write to us at the address below.

Sincerely,

The Editors
Candlelight Romances
1 Dag Hammarskjold Plaza
New York, New York 10017

CHAPTER ONE

Nikki Blake followed the other four tourists out of the creamy gray walls of Fort Charlotte, touching the weather-worn smooth stone with her fingertips. It was like touching history.

Her eyes darted around the high walls of the massive fort on the edge of Nassau, to the solid cannon sighting over them, to the chains where the "bad boys" once were anchored. The guide had told them that, with a twinkle in his dark eyes. He'd taken them down below, down carved stone steps far below the cannon to a smothering hot underground room where kerosene lanterns provided the only scant light. He'd plugged in a trouble light in that small room to disclose a rack with a dummy on it, and one beside it—the tortured and the torturer. Nikki had claustrophobia at the best of times, and the underground room had been trying. When she got back to the surface, she dragged air into her lungs as if it had suddenly gone precious, drinking in the thick, flower-scented subtropical air like a beached swimmer.

She barely heard the guide wishing them farewell as she held on to the cold stone as they went back through the tunnel and out over the moat. It had been an exciting experience, one of many during the two days she'd been on New Providence. She'd needed this vacation badly, but if her aunt and uncle hadn't pushed, she'd probably still be in Ashton having nightmares about that last big story she'd covered for her weekly paper.

"Where to next?" she asked the pleasant tour guide, a mountain of a man in a beautifully colored tropical shirt, as he held the jitney's sliding door open for his party.

"The botanical gardens and the flamingos," he told her with a smile. "The flamingo is our national bird, you know."

She did, but the gardens weren't on her part of the tour. She'd opted for the two-hour city tour, not the four-hour one, thinking that the heat would probably smother her if she had to endure that much of it all at once. Besides, she wanted to go back down Bay Street and wander along the straw market and Prince George Wharf, where the passenger ships docked, and tourists in colorful holiday clothes decorated the view everywhere the eye wandered.

"You're coming, aren't you?" the lady from Chicago asked with a smile. "You'll love the flamingos. And the flowers . . . gorgeous!"

"We've looked forward to it all day," the couple from New Jersey added. "It's going to be great fun."

"I've got some shopping to do," Nikki said reluctantly. She'd enjoyed the group so much. They were all pleasant people, very friendly, not a complainer in the bunch. They'd been good company on the winding tour along the narrow paved roads that led them past stone fences behind which island cattle had once been kept, the governor-general's imposing home and the neatly walled little houses out in the country surrounded by tall casuarina pines, hibiscus, breadfruit, banana, golden palm, and silk cotton trees.

The island had been an incredible experience from Nikki's viewpoint. A native of Georgia, Nikki lived in a medium-sized town south of Atlanta, and the vegetation there, mostly hardwoods like oaks and flowering trees like magnolias and lots of pine trees, was a far cry from these exotic fruit trees.

This was the first holiday she'd taken in the two years she'd worked full time for her uncle's newspaper. It had been a necessary trip, not really a luxury: an escape from the nightmares that haunted her; from the sight of Leda's mud-covered body in the pile of debris the tragic flood had left in its foaming path.

Oddly enough the Caribbean didn't bother her, while the sound of running water back home had brought on horrific nightmares. Perhaps it was the very difference of the place that had begun to soothe her.

Nassau itself was quite exciting, from its busy

11

streets to the fantastic jewel-colored water and coral beaches. Her pale green eyes had misted at her first glimpse of Cable Beach, on the way from the airport to the hotel. She'd never dreamed there could be anything as beautiful as the sudden shock of that turquoise water and white beaches beyond the stand of sea grape and casuarina pines in the foreground. It had literally brought tears to her eyes as she held on to the seat while the rushing jitney swayed to and fro on its winding paved road to the towering white Steel Nassau Inn, a chain hotel overlooking the harbor and one of Nassau's best. Callaway Steel's hotel empire had acquired it several years ago and done extensive renovations.

Everything about the city fascinated her, from the statue of Woodes Rogers and the old cannon at the entrance of a nearby hotel to the story behind them. The people on the busy streets, in the shops, in the hotel itself, were gracious, friendly, proud of their island and their culture. They savored it like aged wine, something impatient tourists had to be taught to do. The first lesson Nikki learned was that in Nassau nobody was in a hurry. Perhaps the subtropical atmosphere had curved time, but the minutes seemed to actually slow and lengthen. Time lost its meaning. The Bahamians moved at a slower pace, took the opportunity to enjoy life a minute at a time, not a day all at once. After the first six hours she spent in Nassau, Nikki put her wristwatch into her suitcase and left it there.

When the jitney let her out at the door of the hotel, she went up to her room and changed into her one-piece white bathing suit with a flowing caftan cover-up in shades of green. The long, carpeted hall was deserted when she opened her door and went back out, with one of the hotel's spotless white towels thrown over one arm. Hotel rules forbade taking towels from the rooms, but Nikki had been too excited to stop and read the signs.

She locked the door behind her and started toward the elevator with the key clutched tightly in one hand.

When she rounded the corner at the elevator, with its huge green palm leaves painted on the metallic walls, the doors were just beginning to close.

"Oh, wait, please!" she called to the solitary occupant, a big, imposing man with faintly waving thick dark hair and eyes that were equally dark and hostile.

He hit the button with a huge fist and stood waiting impatiently for her to get in. She got a brief glimpse of hard features and a square jaw above a very expensive beige suit before she looked away, clutching the forbidden towel tightly against her as she murmured, "Lobby, please."

He ignored her, presumably because he'd already punched the appropriate button. Or perhaps because he didn't speak English. He was deeply tanned and had a faintly French look about him. Nikki had spent the time she'd been in Nassau learning that American-looking tourists were more often than not German or French or Italian. Back home being a Georgian was no distinction, because most everyone else in Ashton was too. But in the Bahamas being an

13

American was a distinction. She smiled delightedly at the irony of it.

"You do know that guests are specifically asked not to remove the bath towels from the rooms?"

It took several seconds for her to realize that the deep, northern-accented English was coming from the man beside her.

She turned and looked at him fully. He was as big as her glimpse of him had intimated, but older than she'd first thought. He had to be in his late thirties, but there was a rigidity about his posture, and those intimidating deep-set eyes, that made him seem even older than that. His face looked as if it rarely smiled, broad and square-jawed and expressionless.

"No . . . nobody said anything yesterday," she stammered. She hated that hesitation in her own voice. She was a reporter; nothing ever rattled her. Well, hardly anything . . .

"There are signs in the rooms," he replied curtly. "You do read?" he added harshly, as if he doubted it.

Her pale emerald eyes caught like small, bright fires under her thick dark eyelashes, as thick and dark as her hair. "I not only read," she said in her best southern drawl, "I can write my whole name!"

She hadn't thought his dark eyes could possibly get any colder, but they immediately took on glacial characteristics.

"Your southern accent needs work," he said just as the doors opened. "Mute the *r*s a little more."

She gaped at his broad back as he walked away. It

14

was one of the few times in her life she'd been stuck for a comeback.

With an irritated toss of her head she bundled the towel up, holding it against her self-consciously as she hurried in her sandaled feet down the long hall, through the patio bar, which was all but deserted in early afternoon, out past the pool, and onto the thick white coral sand where turquoise water and blazing white foam waves lapped crystal clear against the shore.

Arrogant, hateful man to embarrass her like that, to ruin her pleasant mood . . . she'd buy a towel, a big beach towel, at her earliest opportunity, that was for sure.

She dragged up a heavy lounge chair and dropped her towel and hotel key on it, leaving the chair under one of the palm-tiled roof shelters that were scattered around the hotel's private beach.

She dragged the green patterned caftan over her head and tossed it on top of the heap, leaving only the low-cut white swimsuit on her softly tanned body. It was a good figure, even if a bit thin. Her breasts were high and firm, if small, her waist flared out into full, rounded hips, and her legs were long, shapely, and tanned.

She walked carefully in the thick sand past the other sunbathers to the water's edge, wary of those dangerous pull-tabs from canned soft drinks. There were infrequent ones underfoot, despite the valiant efforts of hotel employees who raked the sand constantly to keep it clean.

The water was surprisingly warm, smooth, and

silky against the skin, like those constant breezes near the water that made the sultry heat bearable. Nikki had learned that an hour of walking up and down the streets called for something cold and wet pretty fast. She was constantly scouring the malls and arcades for tall, glass-chunked containers of yellow goombay punch. And she found that she needed to spend an hour at midday lying down in her hotel room with the air conditioner on full. That was something else Nassau boasted—air conditioners at every window. Apparently everyone was vulnerable to the summer heat, not just tourists who were unaccustomed to the subtropical environment.

She moved out into the glorious aqua water with smooth, sure strokes, savoring the sound of it, the sight of tall casuarina pines across the bay, the huge passenger ships docked nearby. The salt stung her eyes with a vengeance, and nagged at a cut on one finger, but it was all so gloriously new and the pace of life was so much slower, that she felt like a small child at a state fair. It seemed odd for her to choose a watery place to relax, after the tragedy that had forced her to take a leave of absence from the paper. But, then, the Caribbean wasn't a river, after all, and the whole environment was so different that she didn't think about anything except the present and the pleasure of new experiences.

Her hair was soaked when her strength gave out and she dragged herself out of the water and back to the yellow plastic-covered lounger to collapse contentedly onto it. She eased up her hips long enough to move the towel, room key, and caftan from under her before she stretched back and closed her eyes.

The peace was something she'd never experienced before. Her life at home was full, and hectic most of the time. But this was incredible. To be totally alone in a foreign place, where she neither knew nor was known by anyone. To have dared the trip by herself, to spend two weeks away from her familiar environment and depend only on herself—she knew already that the experience would last her a lifetime.

All her life Nikki had been told what to do. By her parents until their untimely deaths, then by her aunt and uncle. Even by Leda until her marriage.

Nikki sighed. Leda had been her best friend, and she'd wanted Leda to like Ralley Hall. It had been so important that the two people she loved most would get along. And, of course, they had. A month before Nikki and Ralley were to be married, he and Leda had eloped. They'd been married a year and were planning to move back to Ashton when the flood went tearing through the small house they'd bought. . . .

She was suddenly aware of eyes watching her and she opened her own, turning her head lazily on the chair to find the unpleasant stranger from the elevator standing just at the edge of the sidewalk near the swimming pool, looking out over the bay. He was still wearing his suit trousers, but he'd exchanged his expensive shoes for sandals, and doffed his jacket and tie. He looked relaxed, urbane, and more than a little intimidating to Nikki, whose experience hadn't included high-powered businessmen. She was used to politicians and city officials, because that was her beat on the paper's staff. But she knew the trappings of high finance, and this man had dollar signs printed all over him. He held a glass of whitish liquid with ice and a cherry in it, quite obviously a piña colada, but the favorite island drink hadn't seemed to relax even one of the hard, uncompromising muscles in his leonine face.

While she studied him, he was studying her, his dark, cold eyes analyzing every inch of her body in the wet bathing suit. She boldly gave him back the faintly insulting appraisal, running her eyes over his powerful physique, from massive chest down over narrow hips and powerful legs. He was a giant of a man with a broad face, an imposing nose, a square jaw, and eyes that cut like sharp ice.

Without a change of expression he let his eyes roam back to the turquoise waters for an instant before he turned and walked away, pantherlike, toward the patio bar, without having glanced Nikki's way again. She reached for her cover-up and drew it on, feeling chilled despite the heat. Whoever that man was, he had an imposing demeanor and she wouldn't have liked him for an enemy. But there was something vaguely familiar about him, as if she'd met him before. How ridiculous that was, when except for college and the occasional shopping trip to Atlanta, she'd never been anywhere.

She closed her eyes and lay back on the chair, dismissing the disturbing man from her mind. The whispering surf and the murmur of nearby voices, overlaid by a faraway radio playing favorite tunes, lulled her into a pleasant limbo.

The patio bar was beginning to fill up when she started back into the hotel, but the stranger wasn't anywhere around. She glanced longingly at the bar, where the white-coated bartender was busily mixing drinks. She'd have liked to try a piña colada, but she had no head for alcohol, and especially not on an empty stomach. Supper was going to be the first order of business.

She went back to her room and threw on a sleeveless white dress that flattered her dark hair and golden tan, her brunette hair contrasting beautifully with her unexpected pale emerald eyes and thick black lashes. She wasn't beautiful. She wasn't really pretty. But she had perfect facial bone structure, and a soft bow of a mouth. Her posture was a carryover from ballet lessons, and she had a natural grace that caught the eye when she moved around a room. Her enthusiasm for life and her inborn friendliness attracted people more than her looks. She was as natural as the soft colors of sunset against the stark white sand. But Nikki didn't think of herself as anything more than a competent reporter. When she glanced in the mirror, she saw only a slender brunette with a big mouth and oversized eyes that turned up slightly at the corners, like a cat's, and cheekbones that were all too obvious. She made a face at her reflection before she left the room, looking quickly around for a fringed white shawl to throw over her bare arms before she went out the door.

She was almost to the elevator when she noticed a tall, dark man in a blue blazer, open-throated white shirt, and white slacks coming toward her down the opposite end of the hall. A man with cold brown eyes.

19

CHAPTER TWO

She felt a surge of panic at just the sight of him, and her hand pressed the DOWN button impatiently while she murmured a silent plea that the delinquent conveyance would lumber on down from its third-floor layover before the big man reached her.

But it was still hanging up there when the stranger joined her. He lit a cigarette with a lighter that might have been pure gold from the way his fingers caressed it before he slid it back into his pocket. It might have been gold for all she knew, but obviously money, if he had it, hadn't made him happy. She wondered if he'd ever smiled.

She noticed his eyes on the lacy shawl, and remembering his earlier remarks about the towel, she tugged it closer over the very modest rounded neckline of her dress.

"The curtains," she explained, deadpan. "I had a

few spare minutes, so I ripped them up and made this simply darling little outfit. I'm sure there was a sign, but I read only Japanese," she added flippantly.

He took a draw from his cigarette, looking infuriatingly indifferent. "All the door signs have Japanese translations," he replied coolly. "Japan is rapidly becoming one of the islands' best sources of tourism." His dark eyes measured her body in a way that made her want to cover herself up even more. "You'd look better in the curtains," he added carelessly. "Your taste in clothes is juvenile."

She was gaping at him, open-mouthed, when the elevator arrived, with three passengers speaking rapid Spanish among themselves.

The big man stood aside for her, insinuating himself next to the panel to press the ground-floor button.

Nikki wanted to say something cutting back to him, but for the second time that day she was rendered speechless by her own fury.

"Do you always sulk?" he asked with a curled dark eyebrow.

Pale green flames bounced back at him in a face rigid with dislike. "Only," she replied deliberately, "when I'm verbally attacked by strangers with delusions of grandeur!"

"A kitten with claws?" he murmured, and something resembling amusement made ripples in his dark, deep-set eyes.

"*Gatita,*" one of the Spanish group, a young man, murmured with a wide grin.

The big, dark man threw a look over his shoulder,

21

followed by a rapid-fire exchange of perfectly accented Spanish. Nikki, with only two dim years of the language to go by, understood little more than her companion's *"buenas noches,"* as the elevator doors slid open.

With what she hoped was urbane poise, Nikki moved toward the front entrance of the hotel.

"May I ask where you're going?" the big man asked from behind her.

She stopped as she passed the desk. "To the restaurant on the arcade," she replied involuntarily.

"You're going the long way around," he remarked, indicating a mysterious door across from the elevator, always locked when she'd tried it, which led down a flight of stairs.

"It's locked," she informed him haughtily.

He sighed impatiently. "Didn't the desk clerk give you two keys when you registered?" he asked.

She swallowed. "Yes," she managed weakly, and it suddenly dawned on her which lock that mysterious key was meant for.

"You didn't bother to ask why, obviously," he remarked as she turned and went past him, key in hand, and fitted it into the lock. It opened on the first try.

"I was too busy stealing towels," she muttered.

He followed her down the stairs. "Do you ever read signs or ask questions?" he asked.

She almost laughed out loud. No, she didn't read signs, most of them only said NO ADMITTANCE and a reporter's first duty was to get the story, no matter what barriers got in the way. And as for asking questions, boy, was that one for the books!

"Oh, almost never," she replied with her most southern drawl.

His eyes narrowed as he followed her to the bottom of the steps. "Where *are* you from?"

"Southern Spain," she replied. "*Buenas noches,* you all."

She doubled her pace onto the arcade as she passed the ice cream shop. It, like most of the others, had already closed for the day. There was a sultry, floral breeze and the arcade took on a fairyland quality after dark. The stone benches in front of the coffee shop were deserted, and tourists wandered to and fro around the entrance to the restaurant and lounge on the bay.

The shawl Nikki was wearing did little more than dress up the outfit that arrogant businessman had dismissed as being "juvenile." She didn't need it to protect her from the chill. There wasn't one.

"Do you make a habit of running off in the middle of a conversation?" her elevator companion asked suddenly, moving alongside her without rushing at all. His long, smooth strides made two of hers.

She glared at him. "Were we having a conversation? I hardly think constant criticism qualifies."

He lifted his cigarette to his mouth, and she noticed that the breeze was ruffling his thick, slightly wavy hair, giving him a casual air.

"I don't pull my punches, honey, do you?" he shot back.

She drew the shawl closer while he ground out his

cigarette underfoot. "I very rarely get into brawls," she replied conversationally. "My uncle doesn't think it's ladylike to break people's jaws."

She heard a faint, deep sound that could have been anything. "Doesn't he? How about your parents, young lady, are they mad to let you wander halfway across the ocean alone?"

She drew herself up straight and stared unblinkingly into his dark eyes. "I'm twenty-five years old," she told him. "And I am allowed to cross the street when I want to."

"Hell of a street," he murmured.

"My parents are dead," she added quietly. "I live with my aunt and uncle—it's not uncommon for women to stay at home until they marry where I come from."

She felt his dark eyes on her as they reached the door to the restaurant.

"When did they die?" he asked, placing a huge hand on the door so that she couldn't open it without moving him out of the way—an impossibility.

She studied her sandaled feet. "When I was twelve," she said tightly. Her eyes darted back to his, and before she could erase it, he read the bitter sadness there.

"Have dinner with me," he said shortly, his tone impatient, as if he was offering against his better judgment.

Both her eyebrows went up over emerald eyes. "And be lectured on how I hold my fork?" she burst out.

"Touchy little thing, aren't you?" he asked.

She bristled at him. "Only when I'm being bull-dozed by Yan . . . by northerners." She corrected herself quickly.

One corner of his chiseled mouth quivered, and she could see the smile that died on it flickering briefly in his eyes. "Why don't you say it . . . Yan-kees? All right, I'm from Chicago. What about it?"

"I'm from Georgia. What about that?" she countered. Her eyes glistened with emotion. "And for your information, Mr. Accent Expert, I was born and raised in Georgia, and this accent isn't put on, it's real!"

"How to speak southern in three easy lessons?" he prodded. "Hi, y'all?"

Her mouth compressed angrily. "No wonder they fired off that cannon at Fort Sumter," she breathed. "No wonder. . . . !"

"Peace, Georgia." He chuckled, and something akin to a smile pulled at his hard mouth. "Suppose we raise the white flag over some seafood?"

Her eyes wandered over his broad, hard face. This was insanity. . . .

"Well?" he added curtly.

"All right," she murmured.

He opened the door and ushered her to the entrance of the restaurant, with its huge peacock chairs overlooking the bay where ships and sea gulls caught the eye.

The hostess seated them at a window seat and gave them menus to scan.

"Isn't it beautiful?" Nikki sighed, her eyes dreamy and soft. "Look at the sea gulls putting on a show.

25

It's like watching miniature airplanes do spins and barrel rolls."

"You like airplanes?" he asked.

She nodded. "Very much. I took a few lessons before I ran out of time and money. It was fun."

He glanced at the menu. "What do you see that you like?"

"Oh, the clam plate, please." She glared at him over her menu as she added, "And dutch treat. I buy my own meals."

He cocked an eyebrow at her. "Pardon me, honey, but I don't think your body's worth a whole meal. Possibly not a cup of coffee."

Her fingers crumpled one edge of the menu. "I think I'd like to order another table."

"Stay put. I'll reconsider after I've got something in my stomach. It's been a hell of a day." He shifted to tense and then relax the muscles in his big body.

"If my company is so distasteful, why did you invite me to sit with you?" she asked, taking the battle into the enemy camp.

His dark eyes narrowed. "I was lonely, Georgia," he said quietly.

She felt something leap at her heart and collide with it. "Oh." She waited until the young waitress took their order before she spoke again. "Surely you know people here?"

His broad, square-tipped fingers toyed with his napkin.

"I came down on business," he said. "I don't care for the kind of socializing most of my associates go in for."

She folded her hands primly in her lap, easing back into the unexpectedly comfortable peacock chair that seemed to be the style in the restaurant.

"What kind of business are you in?" she asked.

His eyes darkened, narrowed over a cold smile. "Don't you know?" he asked silkily.

She looked away, ignoring that curt tone as her eyes widened on a newcomer in port. "Look!" she burst out. "Isn't that a battleship?"

He followed her fascinated gaze to a dull gray ship flying a French flag, just steaming into the Prince George Wharf. "An escort frigate," he corrected. "French navy."

"I love the docks most of all," she murmured. "I've never been near a seaport in my life. It's just fascinating to sit and watch the ships dock and steam away. And the way those tiny little tugboats pivot them around in the harbor . . . !" She laughed.

"Are you this enthusiastic about everything?" he asked with a frown.

She glanced at him sheepishly. "It's all new," she explained. "New people, a new environment; I can't help but be enthusiastic about it. This is the first foreign place I've ever seen."

He glanced out the window with a shrug. "I've been here at least a dozen times. It's just another hotel in another city to me."

She drew in a quick, impatient breath. "And that's what's the matter with you," she threw back. "You're too blasé about it. You take everything for granted. Do you realize how many people there are in the world who never leave their hometowns at all?

There must be millions who've never been inside an airplane!"

"They haven't missed much," he grumbled. "Damned cramped places, lousy food . . ."

"I had lots of leg room," she countered, "and the food was delicious. People were nice . . ."

"God deliver me," he groaned. "I invited you here for a meal, not a sermon."

"No wonder you spend so much time alone," she grumbled as the food was placed before them—her clams and his lobster thermidor. She paused to smile at the waitress and thank her, something he neglected to do, before she launched into him again. "You don't like people, do you?" she asked frankly.

His eyes went cold. "No," he replied.

Her wide-spaced emerald eyes searched his across the table. "We're all alike, you know. Lonely, afraid, nervous, uncertain . . ."

"I am not afraid," he ground out. "I have never been nervous. And I didn't get where I am today by being uncertain."

"If you were less hostile," she argued, pausing to chew a mouthful of fresh fried clam and murmur how delicious it was, "people might like you more."

"I don't need to be liked." He sampled his lobster and grimaced. "I swear to God, this lobster would bounce if I threw it on the floor."

"Back home, people are eating hog jowl and corn bread, and you're complaining about lobster," she sighed.

He blinked, his fork suspended in midair. "Hog jowl?" he mumbled.

"Jowl of hog," she told him. "Fat. What poor people have to eat because they can't afford lobster."

He narrowed one eye. "Have you ever eaten them?"

Her face tautened. She lifted another forkful of clams to her mouth. "These really are delicious," she commented.

"And an appropriate dish," he observed, waiting for her to get the point.

She shrugged. "I've been poor," she admitted. "I don't like remembering it, and I don't like talking about it."

"You intrigue me," he said over his black coffee. His dark hands curled around the cup, and she noticed a sprinkling of thick, dark hairs on the backs of them—the same hair that peeked out of his open-throated white shirt under the blue blazer. He had a faintly sensuous quality about him, or seemed to. But she doubted if he knew a lot about women. He was as cold as a chilled wineglass, hardly a ladies' man with that rigidity and lack of charm. He seemed to be a lonely man. . . .

"Are you here by yourself?" she asked suddenly.

"Yes," he said curtly.

She studied the tablecloth. "Married?"

He went absolutely rigid in the chair, his eyes cutting. "Widowed."

"Sorry." She added more cream to her coffee and picked at her french fries. "Well, I've got to get back to my room. It's getting dark."

He stared at her blankly. "Do you change into a statue without sunlight?" he murmured.

29

"Oh, it's not that," she assured him, wiping her mouth with the napkin and throwing down the rest of her coffee. "It's just that I don't like going out at night alone. Too dangerous. Sharks. Man-eating hibiscus. Leering palm trees." She shuddered delicately. Her dancing eyes met his as she gathered her shawl around her and picked up her check. "Thanks for the company. See you around."

"Have you seen the cruise ships by night?" he asked suddenly.

She shook her head wistfully. "They light up, don't they?"

"There's a nice view from the beach. I'll walk out with you, if you like." He stood up, towering over her, and before she could move, he grabbed her check out of her hand and walked away to the cashier.

"You can't . . ." she protested behind him.

But he had his wallet out and the check paid before she could finish the sentence. He held the door open for her and followed her outside.

"And that's why I like southern women," he murmured.

"I beg your pardon?"

"Before you can say don't, I already have," he murmured with a laughing sideways glance. "Slow drawls can be a distinct advantage."

She laughed lightly. "Well, thank you for my supper, anyway."

"You were worth it," he replied.

She stopped in the middle of the sidewalk and turned to him, with her short, dark hair whipping

around her pixie face. "I . . . I think there's something we should get straight."

He seemed to take the thought out of her mouth.
"I've got all the women I need," he replied blandly.
"Of course, if there are ever any openings, I'll keep
you in mind."

She couldn't fish out the reply she wanted, so she
just kept walking.

The beach was deserted, except for one of the hotel
employees who was dutifully raking the sand clear of
debris and a man from the patio bar who was talking
to him. The big man sat down on the concrete sidewalk that led around the restaurant and separated it
from the beach. He motioned toward the wharf.

"They light up like Christmas trees," he remarked.

She studied the huge white passenger ships, fascinated. "I'll bet the passengers do, too," she teased
with a small laugh.

"Would you like a drink?" he asked.

She shook her head. "I never drink with strangers."

His brows ridged upward. "We've just had dinner
together," he reminded her.

"And I don't even know your name."

"Cal," he said after a minute. His eyes went cold.
"If you're determined to pretend."

That remark went right over her head. She was too
intent on the two passenger ships gleaming like ivory
whales wearing strands of diamonds. "I'm Nikki,"
she murmured. "Short for Nicole."

"I think I like 'Georgia' better," he remarked.

She laughed. "You know, back home it's no big thing to be a Georgian. Most folks are. But over here it's unique to be an American, have you noticed? I've only seen a handful of other Americans since I've been here." She glanced up at him. "Do you still live in America?"

"I live in Chicago. But I visit a lot of places." He drew up one powerful leg to rest his arm across. "What part of Georgia?"

"Ashton. In Creek County," she replied. "It's way south of Atlanta, kind of in the middle of the southern part of the state."

"I'm glad you don't write tourist guide maps," he said dryly. "What do you do for a living?"

"Oh, I'm a reporter for—" she began.

"A reporter?" He stood up in one smooth motion, his body taut with rage, his eyes frightening. "My God, I should have known. I thought I was getting the come-on, but I didn't realize I was being had as well. How did you find me?"

She couldn't begin to follow him. "I . . . uh, that is . . ." she stammered, surprised to find herself trembling under the cold, quick lash of his voice.

"Can't you damned vultures find someone else to feed on, without tracking me around the world?" he ground out in a tone that lacerated as surely as yelling would have. "Get off my back, honey, or so help me God, I'll stick you and your damned paper with an invasion-of-privacy suit you won't forget!"

She found her voice and stood up, too, flaring like a torch. "And who are you, anyway, that I'd want to follow you around?" she managed, finding her voice at last.

"You don't know?" He laughed sarcastically. "Who put you onto the deal—Ramond? My God, there's nothing earthshaking about the project, nothing faintly newsworthy to the States. So what do you want, honey? More about Penny? That's a closed chapter in my life, and I'm sick of being questioned about her. Is that clear enough, or would you like it in words of one syllable?"

"I don't have the faintest idea what you're talking about," she said tightly. "You may be some kind of super big fish where you come from, but you're just an oversized tadpole to me, Mr. Big Shot Executive!"

"Sure," he said with cutting contempt. His eyes gave her his opinion of her total worth, and she thought she'd never seen such distaste in a face before. "I don't like parasites. From now on keep out of my way. I don't want to have to breathe the same air with you."

He turned around and walked away, his back as stiff as a starched shirt, and Nikki just stood there, shaking. She sat back down on the ledge until her legs felt more stable, feeling sick and hurt and confused. What did he mean about reporters following him all over the world? Why hadn't he let her finish telling him that she worked for a small weekly paper, not some sensational tabloid? And who was he? Who was Penny? Why did he hate reporters?

For the first time she felt small and vulnerable. More fool me, she told herself with a bitter smile. I should have known better. But what hurt the most was his opinion of her, that he thought she'd picked him up to worm information about some project out of him. She grimaced. How could she have been trying to pick him up when she'd done everything but hire a taxi to keep out of his way? And he'd invited *her* to dinner; she hadn't picked him up. Tears welled in her eyes. He'd prejudged her and hated her on the basis of her profession, without taking time to get to know her, or to give her the benefit of the doubt. And that was what hurt the most. She'd liked the glimpse she'd had of the man inside that hard shell. She had a peculiar thirst to get to know him better. But that wasn't going to be possible now, she knew.

She stood up, wiped away the tears, and started down the sidewalk toward the patio bar. She'd like to have sampled one of those island drinks, like a Bahama Mama or a piña colada. But not at a time like this, when she felt like the end of the world. Drinking was only a crutch for pain, and Nikki didn't like crutches. She swept through the sparsely populated bar on her way upstairs. She wasn't even surprised to find that her dinner companion wasn't among its patrons.

CHAPTER THREE

Nikki went back up to her room overlooking the front of the hotel, and stood quietly by the window, looking out over the struggling air conditioner to the streets below, to the horizon. Instead of magnolia trees there were towering palm trees, making a landscape that seemed alien. It wasn't particularly dark on the horizon, as if the island were perpetually lit up by something other than streetlights or the moon. It wasn't anywhere near the pitch darkness of a Georgia moonless night.

She studied the international grouping of flags over the front of the hotel, recognizing one as British, one as American. All around there were people. Hotel employees called greetings to each other as they passed. Tourists got into and out of cabs at a fantastic rate. And there Nikki stood, all alone, her heart down around her ankles, with that arrogant man's words ringing like chapel bells in her ears. Vulture. Parasite. She was an idealist, believing that what she did with a typewriter might make some small difference in the world. A story about a handicapped child being honored might inspire another handicapped child to try when he or she had given up. A story on an elderly person getting involved in politics might encourage another, more depressed senior citizen to look at life in a brighter way. A story on drugs might keep someone from trying them, might save a life. That was why Nikki wanted to write. Not to get rich. Not to get famous. Only to help.

But how could she expect Mr. Big Shot to understand ideals? She doubted if he even had any, past getting richer. The flags misted and blurred. Who cared, anyway? She didn't.

After a restlessly hot night, during which the valiant air conditioner didn't seem to make even a small difference, she rolled over and turned on Radio Bahamas and listened to a news broadcast followed by a sermon in a delightful British accent, followed by a series of current American top pops and a few golden oldies mingled with the happy calypso beat, the goombay beat, which the Bahamas was famous for. The music made her feel better as it teased her lips into a smile, got into her bloodstream and bubbled. She threw her feet over the side of the bed and got up to dress.

The coffee shop opened at seven each morning, so she hurried down for her egg on a muffin and coffee, and to get ready for another day of sight-seeing. Today she was going on a seashell hunt, on one of those tours she'd learned about at the desk. But first she was going to have breakfast and lie in the sun for a while.

The little coffee shop's trade was brisk. She stood in line for ten minutes, and in exchange for her American currency she got a number of beautiful Bahamian coins and a dollar bill with colorful fish and a photograph of Queen Elizabeth. The money here was as colorful as the scenery, as bright and gay and sophisticated as the people themselves. She was beginning to learn the softly accented English the Bahamian people spoke, to understand their fascinating culture. Each morning now, it had become a habit to go down Bay Street and buy the morning newspaper from the blind vendor near the clothing shop. The elderly gentleman had relatives in the States, he'd told her, although he'd never been there himself. She would press the right amount of change into his hand and he would reply in the West Indian manner, "Thank you, m'dear." Everyone seemed to buy the paper. It was as much a part of the routine as the speedy breakneck traffic of the early morning as workers rushed to their offices and neatly uniformed policemen worked to prevent pileups. The docks were busy, too, as fishermen moved their boats out into the crystal-clear water and the straw market began forming with vendors setting up their stalls with bright native handwork, woven purses and hats and other treasures that were gobbled up by tourists.

"Having a good time?" the girl behind the counter asked her with a grin as she handed her the change.

"I love it!" She laughed back, and the joy of the new experiences was in her eyes, her face, her posture as she danced away toward the tables and came face-to-face with the man from Chicago.

The smile crumbled as she met his cold, contemptuous stare from the table where he was sitting with no breakfast, only a cup of black coffee cupped in his two big hands.

Old habits die hard, and Nikki had been taught manners with her first steps. She gave him a polite, if curt, jerk of her head and made her way to the very back booth, by the door that opened into the back street. She sat down with her muffin and coffee, with her back to the stranger.

It was all she could do to concentrate on her breakfast, which he'd managed to spoil with that steely glare. She was all but shaking with mingled rage and outrage. He knew nothing about her, nothing at all—not that she was conscientious, not that she'd never think of doing anything underhanded to get a story. How dare he judge her! As if she'd write about a horrible man like him, anyway, whoever he was!

"You'll strain your spine if you don't relax," he said from just behind her, causing her to stiffen even more with surprise.

She didn't answer him. She wasn't going to give him the satisfaction of actually replying. She bit into her egg and muffin, which tasted like powdered concrete, thanks to him, and chewed it thirty times

38

before she swallowed. When she took a sip of her coffee, there was no sound to indicate that he'd moved an inch.

Curious, she turned her head and jerked to find him only inches away. He was sitting at the booth behind her, facing the aisle and watching her with eyes she couldn't understand.

"If you don't mind," she said quietly, "I'd like to enjoy what's left of my breakfast."

"There wasn't much of it to begin with," he replied.

"Why don't you go out and take care of your own business?" she asked him coldly. "I came over here for a vacation, not to fight the Civil War after every meal."

She started to get up, unfinished breakfast and all, but he blocked her by stretching a powerfully muscled arm across the booth. She collided with it and felt an electric shock run through her slender body before she jerked back with a muffled gasp.

He didn't like that betraying little movement; his face tautened at it. He laughed shortly. "I'm not used to women running from me," he said. "Especially not women reporters."

"I work for a weekly paper, not a scandal sheet," she said bitingly. "We have a paid circulation of six thousand and we are hardly likely to set the world ablaze with stories on Jim Blalock's fifty-pound cabbage or our new flood-control ordinance."

He studied her face quietly. "A weekly, huh?"

"While we're about it, allow me to blow another hole in your theories," she added angrily. "I don't

39

know who you are. And frankly I couldn't care less. My first impression of you was right on the money. I should have turned around the minute I saw you coming toward the elevator. Next time I will."

She ducked under his arm, tray and all, and stood up.

"All right, I'm convinced," he said, moving in front of her.

"I'm thrilled. Will you get out of my way, please?" she added.

He sighed deeply, taking the tray from her. "We're going to have a rocky relationship if you keep this up."

"You'd be lucky," she returned, but after a minute she sat back down at the table opposite him.

"Not that kind of relationship," he told her. His quiet eyes searched hers. "You aren't hard enough for holiday affairs."

"And you've got all the women you need," she replied with a faint twinkle in her eyes.

"Something like that." He leaned back to light a cigarette while he watched her nibble halfheartedly at her egg and muffin. "Twenty-five is a bit young for me, anyway, Georgia."

"Twenty-six in two weeks," she replied.

There was a long, potent silence between them while murmuring voices from other tables drifted by.

She looked up into dark, searching eyes and felt the breath chased out of her lungs by the intensity of that unblinking stare.

"How long are you going to be here?" he asked gently.

"About ten more days," she managed in a strange little voice. Her heart began to do the calypso in her chest as she returned that long, searching gaze. How odd, it seemed as if she'd known him forever . . .

Strange sensations wandered through her at the piercing quality of his eyes. He was such an uncommon quantity to her. She felt safe and threatened, all at once, and something in that utterly adult look of his made her feel strangely vulnerable. If I had good sense, she thought wildly, I'd break and run and never go near him again until I was safely on the plane home. But she was frozen in place. She couldn't force herself to get up and leave him there.

"Don't start looking for cover," he said, reading the apprehension in her taut features. "You don't need to feel threatened with me, little one."

"I'm not little," she said breathlessly.

"Honey," he said, standing even as he crushed out his cigarette, "compared to me, you're tiny."

She stood up beside him, forced to admit the truth in that bland statement. He loomed over her like some dark giant, as solid as concrete, as powerful as a professional athlete. There wasn't an ounce of flesh on him that wasn't firm, no sign of a beer belly or its upper-crust equivalent. His stomach was as flat as her own, his posture not only proud and arrogant, but full of barely concealed vitality. He'd said he'd been married, and she wondered if there were children. But before she could get her muddled thoughts together, she found herself being shuttled out onto the sidewalk.

"But I was going back to my room," she protested, feeling that warm, strong grip on her elbow as he hurried her across the street.

"What for?" he asked without breaking stride.

"To get my swimsuit on."

"You can't swim on a full stomach."

"But I can sunbathe . . ."

"You'll blister," he remarked, glancing sideways at her creamy complexion against the pale green blouse and white slacks she was wearing. "Or worse, wind up like old leather. Don't fry that perfect skin. It's one of your better features."

"So complimentary," she mumbled. "What do you think you're doing, dragging me along like this?" she added as they dodged other tourists. It appeared that not only did the local people drive on the left-hand side of the road, they walked on the left-hand side of the sidewalk as well. That had caused Nikki quite a few collisions until she got the hang of walking in crowds.

"I'm taking you under my wing," he replied.

"If you did, you'd crush me," she told him. "And besides, it's too early, none of the shops will be open."

"Which makes this the best time of day to explore," he replied, strolling along beside her like a man without a care in the world. The brown open-necked shirt he was wearing was almost exactly the shade of his eyes, dark against the white slacks on his powerful legs. He was a striking man.

"The beach . . ." she began weakly.

"Will still be there when you get back," he promised. "Now shut up. I'm rescuing you from certain boredom."

She gave up, falling into step beside him when he released her arm long enough to light a cigarette and send out a great cloud of smoke.

"Do you always capture people this way?" she asked politely.

"Only when it's necessary." He threw her a mocking look. "It never has been before. It's usually the other way around."

"I don't chase men," she informed him. "I'm only a libber where salaries, working conditions, and rights are involved. I don't want to brawl or press two-hundred-pound weights, thank you." She gave him a brief scrutiny. "I'll bet you think women should be kept in harems and veils."

"On the contrary," he replied. He took another drag from the cigarette, and paused to watch a straw vendor setting up shop on a wide corner as they passed it. "I'm not a chauvinist. The world is changing, and I'm doing my best to change with it." His eyebrow cocked at her. "Although I will admit that harems have their place. God knows what I'd do without mine on cold nights."

"Oink, oink," she murmured.

"Cats, honey, cats. All female, all Siamese. Four of them." He shrugged. "Dogs are all right, I keep one around the grounds for intruders. But it's damned hard to pet a two-hundred-pound Doberman with killer instincts. The cats are friendlier."

"I thought Siamese were vicious," she remarked.

"They fight back," he replied. "But they're loving

43

animals, too. I don't know about you, Georgia, but I can't tolerate people or animals without a little spirit. I hate patronage." His eyes darkened. "God, I hate it!"

She studied his hard face. His gaze was averted, and he seemed to be carved from the same stone the old fort had been. He must be an important man, she decided. He had a quality she'd never seen in any of her contemporaries. Something extra. Magic.

"Is that why you travel alone?" she asked, the words slipping out before she could stop them.

He glanced down at her. "It's one reason. But I don't always travel alone."

A woman. The words flashed into her mind and he read them in her eyes and smiled faintly.

"No, honey, not on a business trip," he murmured dryly. "I'd never be able to think straight with that kind of distraction. I meant, I take Lucifer with me occasionally."

She stopped in the middle of the sidewalk with her mind swimming. "Lucifer?"

"The two-hundred-pound Doberman," he said.

Her eyes searched his. "You said he was a guard dog. Do you need guarding?" she asked, measuring him.

"I can handle myself. But Lucifer is a powerful deterrent, and I have enemies."

"You mean, enemies who might try to kidnap you for ransom?" she asked, all emerald eyes and arched brows.

"Or worse," he agreed. "My, my, what an expression! You are a babe in the woods, aren't you?"

"Cal, what do you do?" she asked bluntly, calling him by name for the first time.

"I'm a businessman," he said vaguely.

"I know, but—"

He lifted a big finger and pressed it to her lips. "Not now," he said gently. "I think I like it better this way for the time being."

"Are you a Russian spy?" she teased. "A Martian scout?"

He chuckled softly. "I'm a hard-working man on holiday."

"You look as though you could use one," she remarked as they walked along the narrow street that ran along the docks. It wasn't really wide enough for cars to park alongside it and still let traffic through, but by some miracle of navigation, the most incredibly large automobiles were able to squeeze through the narrow street. And tourists soon learned how to press back against the buildings to keep from being separated from their toes.

"Isn't this fun?" Nikki laughed.

"Speak for yourself," Cal grumbled, trying to fit his bulk alongside hers as a pink Cadillac slid past them.

"How did you get to be so big, anyway?" she asked him.

"My father was a Dutchman—from Friesland originally, as a matter of fact. A giant of a man from a land of large people. My mother was French."

"How in the world did you wind up in Chicago, then?" she asked, fascinated.

"I was born in the middle of the war," he explained. "My father had left Holland with his division to take part in the Allied invasion of Europe. He met my mother in France. They married and I was born the same year. They came to America because of me, I was told," he added with a dry laugh. "There were no opportunities in Europe after the war, unless you were involved in the black market. My father had the idea that Chicago was as close as he would ever get to paradise. He settled down, got an engineering job with one of the auto makers, made a few minor investments, and let himself be talked into some stock in an oil rig."

"And lost his shirt, I imagine," she teased.

"Not quite." He paused at one of the straw vendors' stalls. "This sun's getting hot. How about a hat?"

"Only if you get one, too," she replied. "I don't want to walk around alone in a hat."

"And you call yourself a reporter," he chided. "Where's your spirit of nonconformity? The hell with what people think. Let them worry about what you think, for God's sake."

She flushed uncomfortably. "I'm an introvert by nature," she admitted reluctantly. "Everything past, 'Hi, my name's Nicole!' is pure bravado."

He searched her soft eyes, smiling. "No one would ever suspect it," he murmured. "You're not a bad actress."

"Then why was I turned down for the lead in our school play?" she asked unblinkingly.

"What was your school play?"

She grinned. "*King Lear.*"

He chuckled deeply. "What was the matter, couldn't you grow a beard?"

"You guessed it." She reached out and touched one of the patterned straw hats, done in royal blue and yellow flowers with green petals and little red buds. "Isn't it lovely?" she murmured.

He picked it up and handed it to her, choosing a plain tan one with no frills for himself. He handed the smiling vendor a big bill and waved away the change and the thanks.

"That was nice of you," she said as they walked away, with her new hat perched jauntily on her dark head.

"You're welcome. It suits you," he added with a grin.

"That, too, but I meant letting the woman keep the change. I asked one of them how long it took to make one of those big straw purses, and she said it was a day's work. Most people like to bargain until they get the price down to almost nothing."

She felt his eyes on her, although he didn't say anything. Perhaps he was remembering what she'd left unsaid in the restaurant last night—that she knew what it was to be without.

"Do you like old things?" he asked suddenly.

"I'm hanging around with you, aren't I?" she replied blandly.

He glared at her. "Old things, madam, old things. How would you like to see a fort?"

"I saw Fort Charlotte yesterday," she recalled. "But I don't mind going again. . . ."

"Fort Fincastle," he interrupted.

47

"Fincastle? Oh, that was the one I didn't get to see," she murmured. "The tour guide didn't want to have to drive up that enormous steep hill. He said it wasn't worth looking at, anyway."

He looked irritated. "It most certainly is. Come on. We'll get one of those picturesque little carriages; you'll like that, it's right up your alley."

"How disappointing that we can't take a jet to it," she returned with a grin. "That would be more your style."

"Keep it up and I won't feed you lunch."

"That," she said, "is blackmail."

"Persuasion," he corrected. "I hope you're up to the climb, you delicate little thing."

"I hope you don't mean we have to do any mountain climbing," she murmured, glancing down at her flat sandals. "These weren't designed for climbing."

"There are steps. Come on, honey, let's get going. I've got a conference at three o'clock with the minister of architecture."

"Going to build something, are you?" she asked.

"Ummmhum," he murmured, scanning the area for the carriages. "A hotel. The biggest and best the out islands have ever seen, complete with hot tubs, saunas, a built-in spa, lounge, and a shopping center."

Strange, he didn't look like an architect. But then, she thought, what did he look like?

He hailed a carriage and helped her in, the conveyance groaning under his formidable weight as he settled in beside her.

"This is how you get the best tours of Nassau," he

told her, and settled back as their driver began to give them a brief history of Nassau, highlighting it with stories of pirates and the first governor, Woodes Rogers, who drove them out and made Nassau safe for its residents.

As they passed the Cathedral Church of Christ, with its beautiful wrought-iron fenced courtyard and masses of tropical flowers in bloom, the guide told them that the first building had been erected in 1670. It was destroyed by the Spaniards in 1684 and rebuilt in 1695. It was destroyed again by invading Spaniards in 1703. The third church, built of wood, was built in 1724 but had to be replaced in 1753 with cut stone. The fifth church, the present one, opened in 1841.

"The tower there," the guide added, "is all that remains of the fourth church."

"It's beautiful," Nikki remarked, and wished they had time to go inside.

"We'll come back," Cal assured her. "The inside is a treat to the eyes."

"You've been inside?" she asked him.

He nodded. But he didn't say anything more, leaving the talking to the guide as they went past a huge silk cotton tree, old buildings, landmarks and flowering hibiscus, bougainvillaea, and towering poinciana trees with their wild orange flowers that lined the way to the fort.

Minutes later the driver pulled up in front of a grove of towering trees with limbs almost interwoven to make an arch leading to a barely visible set of steps far in the distance.

Cal helped her out and took her arm to guide her along. Other tourists were gathered at the base of the steps, and Nikki realized with a sense of smothered terror that along with the stone staircase was a waterfall.

Her voice stuck in her throat as Cal, who had no idea what the sound of a waterfall would do to her, carried her along beside him, murmuring something about a water tower at the top of the staircase.

Nikki felt her muscles contract as they neared the steps, as she saw the water cascading down two levels of stone beside the steps, and the sound of it was like no other sound to her sensitive ears.

With that sound came another—the sound of a flood raging over the earthen dam on the river. The sound of the water breaking it, bursting through in a foaming muddy wall to overwhelm the small houses nearby where twelve people, sleeping, unaware of the dam break, would never wake up again.

They were almost upon it now, the water was everywhere, she saw the television film of the flooding, the muddy debris, Leda's open eyes staring up at her . . .

"No!" she moaned, freezing in place with her eyes mirroring the terror knotted in her stomach.

CHAPTER FOUR

He turned to her, catching her by both arms. "You're pale," he said gently. "What is it—the crowd?"

"The . . . waterfall," she whispered shakenly. "Silly, but I . . . I can't stand it. Please, let me go."

He turned her with one smooth motion and marched her back off to the carriage, where he put her in back and climbed in beside her with the agility of a much younger man, motioning the carriage driver to go ahead.

She felt a big arm go around her shoulders, felt a shoulder under silky fabric against her cheek as he held her quietly, without asking a single question.

They were back in the city before she got her breath again and moved reluctantly away from that comforting arm.

"Which was it, a flood or a hurricane?" he asked shrewdly, studying her face with narrowed eyes.

"A flood," she replied. "Isn't it insane? I don't mind the surf or the beach at all. But if I go near a waterfall or a river, I get sick to my hose."

"Have you talked about it?" he persisted.

"Only to my uncle," she said quietly. "He's edited the paper for fifteen years. Before that he worked on a big city daily as a police reporter. But the job has made him hard. I don't think he really understood what it did to me."

"Suppose we go back to the hotel, get into our swimming gear, and lie on the beach for a while?" he asked. "And you can tell me all about it."

Her pale eyes flashed up to his and locked there. "Your conference . . ."

"Isn't for several hours yet," he reminded her. He searched her troubled eyes. "Hasn't anyone ever told you how dangerous it is to bottle things up inside?"

"I'm . . ." She stared at the passing businesses, the tall hotels. "I'm not used to talking about myself."

"Neither am I, but you've managed to drag more out of me in two days than most of my associates have in ten years." He looked as if that amused him greatly, but his eyes were kind. Dark and full of secrets.

She stared straight ahead at his shirt where the buttons were loose, at a patch of bronzed chest and curling dark hairs. "I could use a swim," she murmured.

"So could I." He chuckled. "It gets hot out here."

"Now, that it does," the driver agreed, glancing

back to make sure his passengers were okay. He hadn't made a remark up until then, but Nikki had sensed concern, and now she saw it in his dark eyes.

"I'm fine," she told him. "Just too much sun, I think."

"You get used to it," he replied dryly.

To the sun, yes, she thought, but how about tragedy? Did it ever completely leave, did the horrible images of it ever fade? She had her doubts.

The beach wasn't even crowded when they laid their towels and robes down on the loungers under the little thatched roof shelter.

Nikki had bought herself a towel in the hotel shop, and apparently Cal had his own—a tremendously big white one with the initials CRS in one corner. She pondered on those all the way down in the elevator. The initials, oil, investments, all of it, added to his unusual parentage, seemed to ring bells far back in her mind, but she couldn't make them into a recognizable melody.

She laid her green caftan on the lounger as Cal stripped off his colorful blue beach shirt. Clad only in white trunks, he was enough to make any woman sit up and stare. His broad chest was powerfully muscled, with a wedge of thick, dark hair curling over the bronzed muscles down to the trunks that covered lean hips and led down to legs like tree trunks. He was the most fascinating man Nikki had ever seen, and she couldn't help the stare that told him so.

53

He chuckled at the expression on her face. "They do wear swimming trunks in Georgia?" he teased.

"Huh? Who?" she murmured.

"Men."

"Uh, oh, yes," she stammered, flushing. She pulled her chair out into the sun and stretched out on it to drink in the warm, bright sunlight.

Cal stretched out beside her on his own chair with a heavy sigh, his dark eyes sliding down the length of her slender body in the clinging white bathing suit.

"That's the only thing I've seen you wear that suits you," he remarked.

She turned her head on the lounger and met his dark, searching gaze with an impact that sent tremors like miniature earthquakes through her body. Without the civilizing veneer of outer clothing he was as sensuous as a cologne commercial.

"I can hardly go around in a bathing suit all my life." She laughed, trying to make her voice sound light.

"That's not what I meant," he replied. His eyes swept over her critically. "That deep, low neckline gives you more fullness, and the color brings out your tan and those fantastic eyes. Your legs are your main asset—long and smooth and delectable."

She swallowed nervously. He made her feel positively threatened. It took every ounce of willpower she possessed to keep from folding her arms across her small breasts.

"Don't look so embarrassed," he said gently. "You've got a good body, small breasts and all, but you could dress it better."

Her face went rouge red. "Cal!" she burst out.

He threw back his dark head and laughed. "My God, talk about repressed areas. . . . Don't you date at all?"

"Well, yes, I do, but most of my dates don't give blow-by-blow accounts of my measurements," she said, exasperated.

"You make me feel a hundred." He sighed musingly.

"How old are you?" she probed gently, her eyes wide and curious.

"Does it matter?" he countered, his eyes watchful.

"No. I'm just curious."

"I'm thirty-eight," he replied, and for an instant time seemed to hang while he waited with impatient interest for her reaction.

"Well?" he prodded shortly.

"What would you like, a rousing cheer?" she asked with arched brows. "Congratulations on having escaped middle-aged spread? An invitation to do a centerfold . . .?"

His face relaxed into a muffled smile, and he laid back down, shaking his head.

"Better watch out," she warned under her breath, "that's the second time you've smiled in five minutes. Your face may break."

He drew in a deep, relaxed breath and smiled a third time. "You make me feel as if I've only started breathing again, Georgia," he replied quietly. "I'm finding light in my darkest corners."

"It's the atmosphere, not me," she denied, stretching. "You just needed a push out the door."

"I'd like to know about the flood," he said after a minute.

She opened her eyes, riveting them to the curling white foam against that crystal-clear aqua water, to the swimmers knifing through the silky water.

"We've had flash floods all my life," she began slowly. "But the dam always kept them from amounting to much. It was sturdy and had withstood floods for forty years or more, so nobody worried about heavy rains. Until three weeks ago," she added quietly. "The dam broke in the night, and water shot over it like water over the falls, one man who saw it happen told us later. Tons and tons of muddy water swept along the riverbed, overflowed, and washed over a subdivision on its banks. One of the victims was my best friend, Leda Hall. I got there," she said, her voice going light, "just as the rescue people were dragging her out of a pile of debris that had lodged under a bridge downstream." Her voice broke, and she waited until it steadied before she spoke again, with images of that horrible morning flashing like specters through her mind. "She was covered with mud, like something barely human. But the worst of it was when one of the neighbors said that they'd heard screams from under that bridge for hours after the impact. I . . . I couldn't stop thinking that she might have been hurt, and in pain . . . but nobody could find her in the dark, you see, in all that debris." Tears rolled down her smooth cheeks. "It haunts me . . ."

He reached over and caught her fingers in his, pressing them gently. "How in God's name did you ever get into reporting?" he asked quietly. "You don't have the emotional makeup for it, honey. You aren't hard enough."

She wiped the tears on the hem of her caftan and laughed wetly. "I'm not good for much, am I? Not hard enough for holiday affairs, not hard enough to be a reporter . . ."

"We could work on that first one," he said in a new, different tone.

She turned to find his eyes tracing the soft lines of her face, slow and dark and sensuous.

"Care for a swim?" he murmured.

She nodded, feeling as if she'd had the floor taken abruptly out from under her.

He stood up, waiting for her to precede him into the water before he followed suit.

They swam lazily for several minutes before he surfaced beside her, slinging water out of his eyes. His lashes were beaded with salty water, and she noticed how thick they were, almost as thick as her own.

"Feeling better?" he asked. Standing on the sandy bottom, he towered over her while she tried to keep both feet balanced in the swell of the tide as a power-boat went past with a roar.

"Much." She nodded. "Thank you."

"For listening?" he asked. "Or for taking your mind off it?" he added with a wicked smile.

So it had been a joke, but she wasn't laughing. She bit off a theatrical giggle. "Oh, it did that."

Before she had the words out, his big hands clamped into her waist and dragged her body fully against his, holding it so that she felt the strength of the powerful muscles crushing her breasts, her thighs. She gasped at the suddenness of the move, at the new angle of seeing his eyes from inches away instead of feet.

"I wasn't teasing," he said quietly. "Could you handle an affair with me?"

She couldn't speak. The contact with his body had drained her strength; the words made oatmeal out of her mind.

"Cal . . ." she whispered shakenly as her eyes dropped to his wide, chiseled mouth and she wondered achingly how it would feel against hers.

"I didn't mean to let this happen," he whispered gruffly, catching the hair at her nape to jerk her head back as he bent. His mouth caught hers before she could react and ground against it with a hard, uncompromising pressure that seemed to burn brands in her mind.

"Don't fight me," he breathed, pulling away enough to brush his lips softly, tantalizingly, across hers until they parted involuntarily. "That's it . . ." he bit off, breaking her mouth open under his, and the world disappeared in swirls of blue and white and pure blinding silver. . . .

His mouth was warm and wise and stirring her senses in ways she'd only dreamed about before. She tasted salt on it, as it demanded response; she felt the powerful muscles of his shoulders tauten as her hands clung to them, her fingers biting into them, her body dissolving against his like melting gold.

He let his lips slide down her cheek to her ear

while his arms crushed her close, letting the sea rock them gently in its watery embrace. She heard his quick, rough breath whisper past her ear.

"It's good between us," he said gruffly.

She licked her bruised lips, her eyes closed against the blinding sun, the radiance of that passionate kiss. She felt incredibly weak. "The people on the beach . . ." she whispered shakenly.

He laughed softly. "They're all stretched out under sunglasses and suntan oil, oblivious to everything. See for yourself." He chuckled, releasing her a little so that she could look for herself.

Sure enough, not one pair of curious eyes had seen them. She couldn't quite look at him. She felt a surge of shyness. Even when she'd been engaged to Ralley, it had never been like this. . . .

"Soft little mouth," he whispered, tracing its slightly swollen contours with one big finger. "I like the feel of it," he whispered, bending to brush his lips softly, briefly against hers. "It's like touching a gardenia petal, smooth and silky and cool against my mouth." He kissed her again, just as briefly, his face beaded with salt water, his body cool where her hands rested on his hard-muscled chest over that curling thatch of black hair.

One hand moved, taking her fingers and working them sensuously into the mat of hair over the silky muscles, in an aching caress.

He drew back and his eyes searched hers while a sudden silence hung between them, warm and sweet and wild.

His chest rose and fell rapidly, and darkness invaded his eyes as she slid her free hand to join the other, discovering the hard, cool contours of that massive bronzed chest with a smoldering excitement. She couldn't recall ever seeing Ralley with his shirt off, or wanting to. But she loved the sight and the feel of this man, the texture of his skin, the tone of the muscles, the faint scent of expensive cologne that clung to him, the magic in those hard, warm lips. . . . She felt as if she were drowning in him, and she never wanted to be rescued.

"Enjoying yourself?" he murmured, watching the lights dance in her eyes, color her cheeks.

With a shock she suddenly realized where she was, whom she was with, and what she was doing, all at once. She drew in her breath sharply, pushing away from him to stare up into his eyes with shamed fascination.

That stare said it all. Something dark and quiet lay in his eyes, relaxed the hard lines of his face for just an instant. He smiled—a slow, smug smile that made him look faintly wicked, and devastatingly attractive.

"I'll race you to the wall," he challenged, narrow-eyed.

"You'll probably beat me, too," she replied, joining in the game. If he wanted to ignore what had happened, she'd go along. It was probably for the best, anyway.

But long after they'd parted company at the elevator, and she was dressing for lunch, she remembered the hunger in that rough kiss. His wife was dead. But had he been a long time without a woman in his life? That might explain a lot. But it was disappointing, too. Nikki ran a brush through her hair with a long sigh. Trust me to lose my head over a man I'll never see again, she grumbled to her reflection. Just my luck these days.

Cal had already told her that the conference would most likely last all day. He was having lunch with his associates, and would probably have supper with them, too.

But he might have time for a nightcap, he'd added, and if he could manage it, he'd call her. She'd smiled and said that was fine, and walked away. But she'd felt like wailing. She hadn't wanted to leave him. She'd wanted to spend the rest of the day with him, sight-seeing or swimming, or just talking. She wanted to learn more about him, what he did, what his life was like. She wanted to be kissed again in that wild, hungry way.

She put her suitcase back in the small closet with a sigh. This must be that second childhood she'd heard about. Ridiculous to get that nutty about a man she'd only known for two days.

She went down the hotel arcade to the chain restaurant for lunch, treating herself to a delicious hamburger and fries and coffee while she watched the sea gulls play over the water.

Next door was the restaurant and lounge where she'd had supper last night with Cal. It seemed so long ago now. They'd learned a lot about each other since then.

61

When she was through, she wandered back down Bay Street and browsed through the shops, her eyes sparkling with curiosity as she saw elegant emeralds, colorful imported fabrics, perfumes, and all kinds of exotic imports. But something was missing. The wonders that had been so exciting before were just routine now. It wasn't the same anymore, being alone.

She thought back to the days before Ralley's interest in Leda became obvious, to things they'd done together. Strange, she couldn't remember Ralley ever enjoying simple things like window-shopping or strolling down streets. He was only interested in football games, noisy parties, and talking shop with other reporters. But at the time, she'd forced herself to like those things, even though it went against the grain of her own nature. Nikki wasn't a sports fan. She hated noise, alcohol, and people who played Russian roulette with mind-warping drugs. Her tastes ran to symphony concerts, the ballet, and art exhibits. Ralley wouldn't have been seen at any of them. She wondered now what they'd ever had in common, besides infatuation. Poor Leda. But perhaps she'd shared those interests, too, as well as being in love with the tall, sandy-haired reporter. Nikki hoped she had. That one year of happiness was all fate had allowed her.

And Nikki had been wary of men ever since. The humiliation of sending out wedding invitations and accepting gifts for a wedding that didn't happen had been a killing blow to her emotions. She wondered if she could ever trust anyone else, if she could believe in love again. Simultaneously, she thought of Cal, and something inside her began to dance.

Nikki went back up to her room around four, ignoring the beach, because if Cal's conference had ended early, he just might call. It could be any time now.

She took a bath and threw on a beige slacks set with a silky brown patterned matching vest. Then she pored through the few paperbacks she'd packed, listened to the radio, stared out the window, paced the floor, and chewed on her nails until six.

In desperation she went down to the restaurant to have supper alone, her eyes restlessly catching on every tall, dark man she noticed on the way. But Cal was nowhere in sight. She rushed through her steak and salad, gulped down her lemonade, and went straight back upstairs, just in case he called. But when seven o'clock, then eight o'clock, came, she began to realize that he wasn't going to call.

He'd said he was busy, but hope had died hard. And maybe it wasn't only business, maybe he did have a woman with him, in spite of his denials. She'd thought when they first met that he was a cold sort of man, with hardly the time to attract women. But she'd revised that opinion drastically. He'd known exactly what he was doing when he'd kissed her. There was no fumbling, no hesitation, about it. He was obviously an experienced man, and far beyond Nikki's small knowledge of men. If anyone had told her a month ago that she was going to allow a stranger to kiss her in front of a beach full of people, she'd have laughed hysterically. But he'd undermined every logical objection she had. And she hadn't fought him. Not at all.

She went back to the dark window and peered out at the streets below. Tourists were still coming and going in droves, and on the street were three young French sailors in their white uniforms with their little red-pommed white caps. She watched them stroll away back in the direction of the docks with a sigh. What would it be like to be a foreign sailor in port, young and single and probably away from home for the first time? She felt a sense of loneliness herself. America seemed a world away from this, and for a moment she missed Uncle Mike and Aunt Jenny. She'd faced all the faint terrors of a tourist alone before the plane landed: What happens if I get hurt, what happens if I get sick, what if someone steals my money and my plane ticket, what if I miss my flight back home . . . and the list went on. But she'd come to grips with all those questions the moment she landed and got her first look at the island from the ground. All the fears had disappeared by the time she got through immigration and customs. She'd worry about it when and if it happened. Not until. And she hadn't had a problem so far.

The phone rang twice before she heard it, and then she made a wild dive across the double bed that left her breathless as her hand made a grab for the receiver.

"Hello!" she burst out.

A deep, slow chuckle came over the line, stopping

her heart just before it ran wild in her chest and brought a sunstruck smile to her face.

"Cal?" she asked.

"I can't think of anyone else who'd call you at this hour of the night," he murmured, "unless your uncle called to check up on you."

"I thought about calling him," she admitted breathlessly, "but I was afraid of the overseas charges."

"It would cost you more to call Atlanta from your hometown and talk fifteen minutes," he replied lazily. "It's not expensive. Join me for a drink?"

"I'd love to," she said sincerely.

"Meet me at the elevator in five minutes." And the line went dead.

She scurried around searching for her shoes, lost one, called it foul names for the minute it took her to locate it, brushed her hair again, checked her makeup, and grabbed her purse. Then she stood watching the clock until four and a half minutes had gone by. She jerked open the door and peeked down the hall.

Seconds later Cal came into view, wearing a tan bush jacket and beige slacks, and she wondered if coincidences like his colors matching hers meant anything.

She closed the door behind her and ran the length of the corridor to meet him at the elevator, her eyes shimmering like jewels underwater, her face slightly flushed, her smile contagious.

"Hi!" she burst out.

He didn't smile. His eyes were narrowed and quiet

and he looked down at her for a long time before he spoke. "It's been quite a while since anyone was that glad to see me," he murmured absently.

She flushed scarlet. "Oh . . . uh, I just didn't want to keep you waiting," she explained.

"Sure." He helped her into the elevator that had just arrived, and punched the ground-floor button.

"Hard day?" she asked.

"Honey, when you're dealing with any government, they're all hard days," he said with a faint smile. He studied her slender body in the beige leisure wear and the smile grew. "Are we reading each other's minds already?" he mused.

She laughed. "I was going to ask you the same thing," she admitted. Her eyes held his shyly for an instant before the elevator doors slid open.

They passed a smiling, nodding group of Japanese tourists as they walked down the long corridor to the patio bar.

"You sounded breathless when you got to the phone," he remarked. "What were you doing?"

"Watching the French navy," she replied dryly. "Wondering what it would be like to go on liberty in a foreign port."

He cast an amused sideways glance at her as they passed the showcase at the entrance to the bar, where artifacts were displayed—like the old cannonball found in Nassau harbor by divers.

"What will you have?" he asked as he seated her by the window overlooking the hedged swimming pool and walkways out behind the huge hotel.

"I can't hold my liquor," she admitted sheepishly.

"So I don't drink anything stronger than wine usually. But I'd love to try a piña colada."

"Had supper?" he asked, and when she nodded, he added, "It shouldn't give you any trouble. Of course, if you try to get up on one of the tables and do the flamenco, I'll do my best to stop you."

She laughed delightedly. When he stopped being the high-powered executive, he was such charming company. She watched him walk to the bar, all rippling muscle and power. Two older women sitting at a table across the room watched him unashamedly, whispering back and forth, and Nikki couldn't blame them for those intent stares. She liked looking at him, too.

He was back minutes later with two tall, frosty glasses full of a milky substance with cherries in them.

"A piña colada," he said, handing hers to her as he took the seat beside hers. "Coconut rum, milk, pineapple, dark rum, and a cherry."

She sipped it and her eyes grew wide. "It's very good," she said, surprised. "I thought it would be bitter, but it's faintly sweet."

"Liquor doesn't have to taste like medicine, you know." He chuckled. "And in this heat, a 'tall, cool one' is almost de rigueur at the end of the day."

She took another sip and sighed contentedly, her eyes going past him to the flower-scented breeze shifting in through the open sliding doors onto the patio with its neat little white wrought-iron tables.

"We can sit outside if you'd rather," he suggested.

She was on her feet almost before he finished the

sentence. "I was hoping you'd say that," she said, leading him outside into the delicious-smelling breeze. The bay was just visible through the palms and sea grape trees and the hedge around the huge swimming pool.

Cal seated her again and settled down into the chair on the other side of the small table, idly watching the waves curling white and foamy onto the beach beyond.

"Peace," he murmured. "I'd almost forgotten what it was. You've made me slow down, Georgia."

"I just pointed your eyes toward the sights." She laughed. "You slowed yourself down. Mmmmmm, isn't it lovely here?" she asked, closing her eyes to savor it all. The wind ruffling her hair, the scents, the faint buzz of conversation from inside the bar, the swish of the palms.

"It reminds me of Miami," he said.

She opened her eyes and took another sip of her drink. "I've never been to Miami," she remarked. "Mike and Jenny—my aunt and uncle—flew down for some convention not too long ago. They said it was hot."

He chuckled. "In more ways than one," he murmured. "And crowded. And maddening to get around in. I'd rather take my chances on New York."

"I've never been there, either." She sighed. "I guess before now, the farthest away from home I've ever been is Daytona Beach. And all I remember about it is sun and sand and Leda pushing me in the swimming pool at the hotel with my clothes on." She

68

smiled at the memory. "She was so much fun, always into something . . ." The smile faded and she took another, longer swallow from the glass.

"Don't look back," he said gently, meeting her eyes across the table.

"It's hard . . ." she said tightly.

"It gets easier," he countered. "Take it one day at a time."

"Just like that?" she asked.

He reached across and touched her fingers with his. "Exactly like that."

The touch of those warm, hard fingers made her tingle with sensations she hadn't felt since he'd kissed her. She studied the back of his hand, the darkness of it sprinkled with crisp, curling hair, the fingers broad and long.

"Look at me," he said curtly.

She raised her eyes to his and found him watching her. His fingers brushed against hers sensuously, lightly teasing them until they trembled, caressing the soft length of them until they parted and began to respond.

Her lips parted at the awesome surge of emotion the simple action ignited. Her fingers arched under the brush of his, and his parted them, easing slowly, sensuously between them in a silence that seemed to cancel out the world and every single thing in it.

He contracted his hand so that it was palm to palm with hers, with all five fingers securely interwoven, and pressed it hard and close while his eyes teased hers.

"Your heart's going like a watch," he murmured lazily. "I can feel it."

"You're not playing fair," she whispered breathlessly. "It's like shooting ducks while they're asleep."

His fingertips were at her pulse, feeling the rough rhythm of it, and his hard mouth was pulled up at both corners.

"Wrong, honey," he said softly. "I'm not playing at all."

She tried to catch her breath, but there was magic in the clasp of that big, warm hand and she couldn't have torn hers away on penalty of death.

"I don't think I could handle it," she protested weakly, her eyes frankly pleading.

"What?"

"An affair," she whispered.

He lifted her hand in his and ran his lips over the back of it with a slow, sensuous pressure. "You've got ten more days to think about it," he murmured. "While I put on the pressure," he added with a wicked grin. "And to pass along a trite expression, 'if you think this is my whole routine . . . ' "

"What . . . what about your business meetings?" she asked.

"Let me worry about that. Finish your drink. You'll need an early night."

"Why?" she asked, grateful for small miracles when he let her hand go so he could finish his own drink.

"I'll tell you in the morning," he said mysteriously.

Her mind was working overtime all the way out of

the lounge. He was interested in her, that was obvious. But she couldn't handle an affair with him, she couldn't. On the other hand, what if he had something more permanent in mind? What if they spent a lot of time together, and he decided that he couldn't live without her? The thought was pure delight. To live with him. To get to know him. To belong to him, and have him belong to her, permanently. She glanced up at him as they walked. It couldn't happen this quickly, could it? People didn't get involved so quickly. But she had. She had!

They were just passing the desk when the clerk called out, "Mr. Steel? Mr. Callaway Steel? There's a message for you."

"Thanks," he said. "Wait for me," he told her as he strolled toward the desk.

Nikki stood there like a young fawn confronted by her first hunter. Callaway Steel. More accurately, Callaway Regan Steel, founder and president of the Steel companies, which included such diversified interests as oil, construction, real estate, and a hotel empire of which this very hotel was a part. More than one national magazine had featured the first-generation American whose uncanny business sense had amassed a fortune from some old oil shares and two small filling stations.

But that wasn't all Nikki had read about the tycoon. His wife had supposedly suffered a fatal stroke soon after the accident that killed the couple's young daughter, Genene. But one tabloid had brazenly called it a suicide resulting from heavy drug use. All that was two years and more ago, but the press still hounded him, because he was always in the middle of some big business venture. Callaway Steel made headlines wherever he went. And this latest construction project and merger talk would do it again, she was sure.

Her eyes followed him, sad and lost and haunted. Something deep inside her began to wither, like a delicate flower cut off from water and sunlight. There had been such promise in the seedling of their relationship, such gentle hope. And now that was at an end. She was as far out of his league as a B-team football squad was from the Dallas Cowboys. She could never fit into his world, into his life, with all those differences to separate them. And an affair would certainly be all he could offer her, at best. He'd said often enough in print that he'd never marry again.

The evening had held such promise. And now it tasted like warmed-over ashes in her mouth. She saw him nod as he listened to the tall young clerk, turn and walk back toward her with a satisfied look on his face. Another business triumph, she thought bitterly. For business was his life now, the only thing that seemed to make him happy.

He stood just in front of her for a minute, reading the sadness in her face, her eyes, and his eyes narrowed in a movement strangely like a wince.

"You really didn't know, did you?" he asked gently.

She turned and went to the elevator silently, pressing the UP button with a slow, steady finger.

"It's been a long day for me," she said quietly.

"Thank you for the drink, but I'd better go on up now."

He caught her arm and turned her toward him. "It doesn't matter," he said shortly. "Look at me, damn it!"

She raised her wounded eyes in self-defense. "Doesn't it?" she asked, her voice faintly trembling.

The elevator doors opened to let a party of people out—the same Spanish-speaking group that had ridden down with them once before. One of the men called a greeting to Cal, who returned it politely, but without enthusiasm.

He let her into the elevator first and joined her, his face hard, his dark eyes stormy under a wide swath of dark hair that had fallen out of place onto his forehead, giving him a faintly roguish air.

"Will you listen . . . ?" he began.

"Oh, do wait for me," a small, very cultured voice interrupted, and a tiny, elderly lady in a very sedate navy and white suit joined them. Her elegant designer scarf matched the deep blue of her eyes and highlighted the bright silver of her hair. "I thought I was going to get left behind, and I do hate being alone in the lobby at night," she added cheerfully, ignoring the undercurrents between the elevator's only other two occupants. "I'm from Tallahassee," she told them. "Florida, you know," she added. "I just adore the islands, they're so . . . different. Now, my son would love this. I only wish I could have brought him with me, but he was so busy. . . . Where are you two from?" she added with a tiny pause of breath.

"No hablo ni una palabra de inglés," Cal said in

73

perfect Spanish, and with a faint smile. *"Pero me gusta Nassau por su siempre brillante sol y cielo azul, y mi mujer le gusta también. ¿Y usted?"*

The small woman smiled sheepishly, nodded, and replied, "Nice to have met you!" in a loud voice, as if she expected foreigners could only understand English if it was yelled at them.

As the elevator doors opened on the first floor, she moved out of it quickly, nodding and smiling, and looking relieved as she moved off down the hall.

Nikki, who'd been watching the byplay with niggling amusement, darted a glance at Cal.

"What did you tell her?" she asked curiously.

"That I didn't speak English, that I enjoyed the sun and sand, and that you did, too." He ran his eyes down her slender figure. "And that you were my woman," he added.

Her face flushed. "Oh, no, I'm not," she said under her breath. The elevator stopped and she ducked past him to get out. "Not now, not ever, Mr. Tycoon. Just put me down as one of your few failed acquisitions."

"And that's something I won't do," he replied, following her down the hall to the door of her room.

She put the key in and turned it, her head bent, her shoulders sagging, her throat filled with tears.

She felt his big, warm hands resting heavily on her shoulders, pressing, holding.

"So I've got money," he said, as if he were searching for the right words, his voice deep and low in the deserted hall. "It pays the bills and supports a few workers. I can go first class when I please, I can afford to run a Rolls and buy a town house in Lincoln Park. But I work hard, Georgia. None of it came easy, and I wasn't born rich. I worked for every dime I've got. I think that entitles me to enjoy a little of it."

She turned, her back to the door, and looked up at him sadly. "Oh, I didn't mean that," she said defensively. "I've read about you, I know what a rough road it was to the top. You're quite a success story. But you and I are worlds apart," she added, feeling it was important that she make him understand what she was saying. "Cal, my people have been farmers for three generations. Not plantation holders, not rich people. Except for a fourth cousin who made a million selling lightning rods, I don't even know any rich people. I . . . I can't cope . . ."

"You've been coping," he shot back. His eyes darkened in that broad, hard face. "My God, you're the first woman I've ever met who ran the other way when she knew my net worth. Don't you want a mink or a new Ferrari?" he added, his voice lightly teasing.

Her lower lip trembled with sheer fury. Her hand lifted and he caught it, taking it to his chest.

"No, mink wouldn't suit you, would it?" he asked softly. "Neither would strands of diamonds or sports cars. You're a wild-flower girl. Daisies and jonquils in carpeted meadows, and the wind in your hair."

She caught her lip in her teeth, trying to stem the tears. She loved those flowers; she picked bouquets of them in season and made arrangements for the

75

table. Ralley had never thought of her that way. He hadn't really considered who or what she was; she'd been more a possession than a person to him.

His fingers went to cup her oval face, holding it up to his dark, gentle eyes while he studied her in a silence rich with emotion.

"Nikki," he murmured deeply, savoring the name on his lips. "Nicole . . ."

"Cal, it won't work . . ." she whispered shakily.

"We'll make it work," he whispered as he bent toward her, taking his time about it, fitting his mouth exactly to hers until it touched gently every single curve of her quivering lips. "Kiss me, Nikki," he murmured against her mouth, and she felt his big arms swallowing her as the kiss made a mockery of every other caress she'd ever known. There was a strange tenderness in him as he explored her mouth, a treasuring of it as if it was a fragile, delicate thing that he mustn't be too rough with. He drew back far too soon and Nikki saw the turbulence she was feeling mirrored in his wood-brown eyes.

"I hope you're properly flattered," he said gruffly. "It's been one hell of a long time since I've been that careful with a woman's mouth."

She was still working on words. Her eyes, her mind, was full of that dark face above her that had suddenly and unexpectedly become her world. "You're very experienced," she whispered.

"What did you expect? A computer with hands?" he asked dryly. "I was married for twelve years, and I wasn't a saint when I proposed." His face clouded. "Nor since," he added roughly.

"I'm not a sophisticated woman," she told him with a voice that felt sandpapery. "I come from a relatively small town, I've never been a partygoer, and I hate what I know of socializing. Cal . . ." She let her eyes drop to his broad chest. "Cal, I don't think it would be a good idea for me to get . . . involved with you."

He tipped her face up to his with a long, broad finger. "Honey, you're already involved," he said quietly. "So am I. And we're getting in deeper by the minute. I touch you, and I tremble like a boy, haven't you noticed that? The same thing happens for you. I'm thirty-eight years old and I've never felt that way before. Don't expect me to walk away from you at this stage."

Her face contorted with indecision, with longing. He was right, he affected her exactly the same way she affected him, but she couldn't make him understand what she was talking about. She'd be winnowed out of his society in less than a week; she wasn't strong enough for the kind of people he associated with. She knew nothing about big business, less about entertaining, and she'd only be a hindrance to him. Physically they were beautiful together, but Nikki had seen too many of her friends' marriages collapse from too much emphasis on the bedroom and too little on the living room. Without a foundation of common interests and friendship that physical side of a relationship, while wonderful, would never sustain the relationship alone.

"Cal, I'm so confused," she whispered, looking up at him with all her doubts in her eyes.

He drew in a deep, long breath. "Give it time, Georgia," he said, lapsing back to her nickname and the earlier comradeship, his smile kind. "Suppose we spend those next few days just getting acquainted? No heavy petting, no passion on moonlit beaches, no sex, period. And then we'll go from there. Well?"

"I want to," she admitted wholeheartedly. Her hands moved unconsciously on his broad chest over the shirt. "Oh, I want to very much."

"None of that, either," he murmured, stilling her hands. "You did say you couldn't handle an affair with me, and I've got a low boiling point. No fair turning up the heat."

She laughed softly. "All right."

He bent and brushed a gentle kiss against her smooth forehead. "Go to bed. Tomorrow I'm going to rent a car and show you the island. Maybe we'll fly over to Freeport and take in the sights, too."

"I'd like that," she replied, her face beaming.

He watched her, faintly smiling. "Sunshine," he murmured. "Daisies will always remind me of you from now on. You're so natural, Georgia. Nothing false, nothing put on, just a vibrant enthusiasm for life. I've never known anyone like you."

"I've never known anyone like you," she replied, studying him. "Cal . . ."

"Don't start that again," he said. "You make feel like a walking checkbook when you look at me like that. I'm a man, Georgia."

"You sure are," she said with a stage sigh, batting her long eyelashes at him.

He chuckled softly, removing his hands from her

waist to jam them into his pockets and stare down his imposing, arrogant nose at her. "I'll pick you up at seven sharp."

"I'll be ready." She opened the door and went inside, smiling at him through the wide crack. "Good night, then."

He smiled back. "Good night. Lock that door," he added firmly.

"Yes, sir!" She got a last glimpse of his amused eyes before she shut the big door and locked it noisily.

CHAPTER FIVE

The next day seemed to go by in a haze as Cal chartered a plane and took her to Freeport on Grand Bahama. She held tightly to his big hand while they wandered through the shops in the International Bazaar and ate in one of the many restaurants there. He bought her a tiny jade elephant, the only thing she'd willingly accept, and she knew she'd treasure it all her life.

Freeport was more spread out than Nassau, with wide boulevards and more sense of space. But privately Nikki liked Nassau best, perhaps because it was more crowded.

"Tired?" Cal asked on the way back, watching her stare down at the turquoise water as they approached the Nassau airport.

"Tired, but happy," she replied, turning to smile up at him. "It was lovely."

"And it's not over," he said with a slow smile. "Feel like some more walking?"

I could get up off my deathbed to walk with you, she thought, but all she said was, "Yes, I do. Where are we going now?"

He stretched lazily. "I thought I'd show you the inside of that church you were so fascinated by." He caught her hand and wrapped it up in his, sending tingles of sensation down her arm. "Then we'll go lie on the beach until it's time for my next meeting."

"Another one?" she asked.

He only laughed. "Honey, my whole life is one big round of meetings, everything from civic ones to board meetings. I don't have time to curse my cats when I'm back in Chicago."

"Do you eat out all the time?" she asked, curious about his life-style.

"I have a housekeeper—a wiry, little white-haired thing who can run circles around me," he said with a smile. "Her name's Maggie, and her specialty is giving me hell when I skip dinner."

"A paragon." She laughed.

"Not quite." He scowled. "Maggie has a tongue that waggles at both ends, as the saying goes. That's her only fault, but she's easy to get to, for the press. I almost fired her over that trait once."

She'd have bet it was after his wife's death, but she didn't ask. Prying into old hurts wasn't her privilege.

"Do you ever relax?" she wondered.

He shrugged. "Business isn't work to me, it's play. I enjoy a challenge."

"Is that what pushes you?" she teased lightly.

His face clouded and froze over. "Not quite." He released her hand and reached in his pocket for a cigarette, realized the plane was about to land, and put it back again.

"Buckle up, honey, we're going in for a landing," he said curtly.

She did as he asked without another word. She'd offended him, without realizing it. His motivation was surely in some way linked to his dead wife and daughter, and she regretted deeply that unthinking question. Her eyes turned toward the window and she didn't open her mouth again.

They went back to the hotel first, to give Nikki a chance to change into more comfortable clothes before they went out again. While they were there, Cal exchanged her room and his for a suite of rooms overlooking the bay.

"Don't get any ideas about seducing me, either." He chuckled as he carried her bags into her bedroom. "I've got protection. Genner!"

A tall, graying man with friendly eyes and a taciturn face came ambling out of the sitting room that connected her room with Cal's. "Yes, sir?"

"Genner, this is Miss Blake. Nikki, Genner has been with me for over fifteen years. He smooths the bumps, makes me eat when I don't want to, and manages somehow to survive four female Siamese cats who hate him fiercely."

She laughed. "How do you do, Mr. Genner?" she said politely, extending her hand and having it lightly shaken.

"Fine, thank you, miss," he replied. "Would you like some coffee, sir?" he asked Cal.

"That might be a good idea."

"None for me," Nikki said quickly, feeling the heat more than ever, even in the air-conditioned sitting room. "I'd like to lie down for a minute or two, if you don't mind."

"Go ahead," he said gently. "I've got a mountain of work to get through and a meeting on the agenda . . ."

Nikki thought guiltily of all the time he'd been spending with her instead of his business. "Cal, if you'd rather put the church off until tomorrow, it's fine with me," she lied.

He shifted restlessly, his big hands jammed in his pockets. "I could use a little extra time to study the proposals on that real estate I need for the new hotel," he murmured.

She pasted a smile on her face. She'd had the morning with him, after all—why should she expect any more.

"Then take it," she said. "I'm really worn out, but I didn't want to say anything and hurt your feelings. You've been so kind . . . about the room and all . . ."

He glared at her. "It wasn't out of kindness and you know it," he growled. "I please myself, no one else."

"You know what I mean," she said gently. "I don't mind about this afternoon. Really, I don't."

He looked hunted for an instant, his eyes pained, his expression one of a man combating a host of conflicting emotions. "I'll call you in the morning, then," he said after a minute.

"That will be fine," she assured him, forcing herself to be cheerful. She glanced around the room. "Why are you staying here in a regular suite?" she added, curious.

Both dark eyebrows went up. "Why not? I own it. I can find out more about its operation from one of the standard rooms than in the executive suite, can't I?"

"Everybody knows who you are, anyway." She laughed.

He shrugged. "It's a well-run hotel," he admitted. "I've known associates to send servants down here with bankrolls to see how efficient the service in their hotels was."

"And . . .?" she asked. "Have you done that?"

"There's never been a complaint," Cal said with a ghost of a smile. "It isn't the newest hotel on the island, but there's been extensive renovation and remodeling, and the service is second to none."

"I'll agree with that wholeheartedly." She nodded. "It's well run, all right. But why build another hotel . . ."

"Not here," he said. "On one of the out islands," he added. "But that's privileged information right now, Georgia."

She nodded. Her eyes flashed up to his and down again. "Well . . . I'll see you in the morning. Or sometime," she added with a smile and a careful carelessness. It wouldn't do to have him think she was begging for his company. Especially now that

84

they were in adjoining rooms. What more did she want?

He nodded, his eyes narrowed and an absentminded look in them. "Sure. Don't go out at night by yourself," he threw over his shoulder.

"Oh, I wouldn't dream of it," she said.

She went into her room and closed the door behind her. It was silly to cry, but she did.

A cool bath made her feel better. She dressed in white slacks and a sleeveless, V-necked white blouse before she went back out again, in search of the little church.

If only she had someone to talk to, someone she could ask for advice. It would be better if she got on a plane and went home right now, before she got in over her head with Callaway Steel. Apparently he was having second thoughts of his own, because he wasn't all that anxious to spend any more time with her. He'd actually seemed relieved when she suggested parting company.

She sighed, walking along the crowded sidewalk, oblivious to her surroundings. She must have really gotten to him with that remark about what pushed him, and it had been a wholly innocent one. She hadn't meant to dig at him, but perhaps he was used to people who dealt in that brand of sophisticated knife-turning.

That kind of loss would be hard to take, those two tragedies so close together. Perhaps he blamed himself. He wasn't a man at peace with himself, nor a man who enjoyed life to any great degree. She suspected that if it hadn't been for his businesses, he wouldn't have made it through until now. The pressure of daily decision-making had probably saved his sanity.

But what kind of life was it? He'd admitted that it had been a long time since he'd slowed down enough to notice his surroundings, since he'd been able to smile. She was glad she could do that much for the tycoon. But it was the man who interested her, despite the gaping difference in life-styles that separated them. She'd wanted very much to get to know him, and she knew now that wasn't going to be possible. Callaway Steel preferred people at arm's length, and that was where he planned to put Nikki, despite the closeness they'd shared last night. It must have been the moon and the rum, she thought sadly. Because in broad daylight, Cal had eyes only for the Steel companies.

She stopped at the door of the Cathedral Church of Christ, her eyes riveted to the worn stone building with its windows that opened from the bottom and swung out, the courtyard with a black wrought-iron fence and hibiscus blooming profusely inside it. It was the most beautiful church she'd ever seen, its history sweeping and fascinating.

The interior had a sweeping grace of design, with high ceilings and ceiling fans, mahogany pews, and white columns. The walls were lined with marble plaques in memory of deceased persons dating back far into the 1800s. One sad one read, SACRED TO THE MEMORY OF LOUISA, WHO DIED 6TH JUNE, 1856, IN THE 25TH YEAR OF HER AGE. Another marked the deaths of the crew of a British ship: crewmen aged sixteen through twenty-nine who succumbed to yellow fever in 1862. Besides the plaques there was an RAF Book of Remembrance listing the officers and men of the RAF who died in performance of their duties while stationed in the Bahamas during World War II from 1939 to 1945.

The silence inside the church was reverent, made more so by the memorabilia of those who had lived and died in the islands so long ago. Nikki wandered down the aisles between the pews, reading the markers, reflecting on what the lives of those people had been like, whether they had been happy or sad, what accomplishments they'd left behind them.

It was a reminder of how fleeting life was, and she remembered Leda, whose twenty-five years had ended so suddenly and so tragically. No one ever expected to die. Death came like a winter storm, so silently, so suddenly.

She clutched her purse tightly in her fingers, staring blankly toward the altar as she remembered, graphically, every minute of the flood she'd covered, Leda's body, the frantic efforts of the rescue people to work around the clutter of reporters and cameras and microphones. It was reminiscent of another flood Nikki's uncle had covered in the mountains, when a dam burst in a heavy rain and shot over a waterfall, killing a number of people, mostly children. That graphic coverage, and the vivid details that had been too horrific to print, had haunted her. The flood that claimed Leda had been added to the other one in her mind, and the memories combined had caused her some serious problems with her emotions.

But now for the first time she felt at peace with herself. This little church was easing the pain in unexpected ways. Perhaps it was the realization that she wasn't alone in grief as she read the wording of some of the plaques, which had been erected by grieving family members and friends so many years ago. Grief was like an heirloom passed down from one generation to the next, and there was no escaping it. One simply had to accept death as a fact of existence, and accept equally the certainty of something better past that invisible barrier that separated life from death. A wisp of verse from Nikki's Presbyterian upbringing lightly touched her mind as she stared toward the altar. ". . . God cause his countenance to shine upon you, and grant you peace."

Tears welled in her eyes and overflowed, and the tight knot of pain inside her seemed to melt away with the action. Now she could heal. Now at last she could live with it.

She turned, dabbing at her eyes with her hand. She never seemed to have a handkerchief or a tissue when she needed it most. She was almost even with the entrance when a shadowy form took shape just inside the door, as she blinked her eyes to force the mist out of them.

"Cal!" she whispered in disbelief.

He shifted restlessly from one huge leg to the other. "I was halfway through a bid when I remembered those," he said quietly, nodding toward the plaques on the walls. "I had a feeling they'd bother you."

She remembered his own losses, his wife, his young daughter, and the tears burned down her cheeks.

He moved forward, pulling out a handkerchief to give her. She pressed it to her tear-filled eyes, catching the scent of expensive cologne in its white softness.

"I'm sorry," she whispered, looking up at him with wide crystal-clear eyes. "You hurt, too, don't you?" she whispered, almost afraid to say it.

His face hardened, darkened. He looked away from her, down the long aisle. "Yes," he said harshly. "I hurt."

And he'd thought about her. He'd cared enough to come and see about her, despite his business. She wanted to bawl over that concern, but she forced her scattered emotions back together, sniffed, dabbed at the last of the tears, and handed him back the handkerchief.

"I'm glad I came here," she told him, moving past him toward the outside again. "I needed to."

"What denomination are you?" he asked as they moved into the light, and Nikki blinked at the sudden brightness against her sensitive eyes.

"Presbyterian," she murmured.

"Now that," he said with a sideways glance, "is a true coincidence."

She stopped and looked up at him. "You aren't Presbyterian?"

He pulled a cigarette out of his blue-patterned shirt pocket and lit it. "My mother was Roman Catholic. My father was a staunch Calvinist. By some miracle they managed to live together long enough to be convinced that neither was going to convert the other. They became Presbyterians in an attempt to find a common ground."

"That's incredible." She laughed.

"So were they," he returned, his dark eyes soft with memory. "A happy couple."

"Are they dead now?" she asked gently.

"My father is," he replied. "My mother is still very much alive. She's in a nursing home, a good one, and she plays a mean game of chess."

"Do you look like her?"

"My father was blond and blue-eyed," he remarked with a wry grin. "I get my size from him. But the rest is Mother."

"Not quite all of it, surely," she remarked dryly, and then flushed wildly when she realized what she'd said.

Laughter tumbled out of him like wine out of a carafe. "Sheltered little country girl . . .?" he murmured with a wicked glance.

"Why don't you go back to your bids and your business?" she muttered.

"Hell, I tried. You got in the way." He took a long draw from his cigarette as they walked. "Let's go enjoy the sun for a while. All I've managed to do is give myself a headache."

She smiled. Suddenly the day began to take on a new radiance.

They went to a casino over on Paradise Island that night, where Cal taught Nikki the art of gambling.

She'd never even played poker before, and she didn't have a high opinion of gambling in any form, but there was an aura of glamour that clung to this exclusive place.

While the roulette wheel spun and spun, her eyes darted restlessly around the room, finding every sort of wearing apparel imaginable, from evening jackets to sport shirts and everything in between. It was the most fascinating place she'd ever been, despite the fact that she was wearing a long coral-patterned gown when most of the other women were in short dresses or elegant pant suits. But Cal was wearing an evening jacket and a black tie with his white silk shirt, and Nikki had garnered enough courage over boiled lobster earlier that evening to tell him how devastating he looked.

He'd given her a strange look over that remark, one she couldn't puzzle out. She had the feeling he never knew whether or not people were lying to him, because he was rich. And she was suddenly glad that she wasn't.

"You won," he said into her ear, distracting her from the people-watching habit reporting had ingrained in her.

"Oh, I did?" she murmured vaguely, and asked how much.

He told her, and grinned at the stunned expression on her face.

When they cashed in the chips, she handed half a year's salary to him, which produced an expression that was a cross between incredulity and disbelief.

"What the hell are you handing it to me for?" he asked. "You won it. It's yours."

"Oh, no, it's not, you staked me. Here." She caught his big hand and pressed the wad of notes into it.

He stared at it as if it was a dead fish, lying green and lifeless on his palm. His deep-set eyes stared down into hers searchingly. "I assume you aren't independently wealthy, if you work for a newspaper?"

She smiled. "No. My uncle owns the paper, and I wouldn't starve, but my parents didn't leave me anything substantial."

"Then why turn down a sum like this?"

She stared down at it and shrugged. "I don't know. Maybe because it came too easily. I like working for what I get." She tilted her head up at him. "You know, I've seen men go to carnivals and spend a week's salary tossing nickels and dimes for plates they could have bought for a dime apiece. The fever gets into them and they won't quit, and maybe they've got two or three children and a wife at home who'll have to suffer because of that gambling impulse. I may sound idealistic, but I've no use for gambling. Maybe here nobody goes hungry if a player loses two or three thousand dollars. But I've seen the other side of the coin, and it's not pretty."

"You might consider donating it to charity," he suggested.

Her eyes twinkled. "I've got a better idea. Why don't we both donate it to that little church we visited?"

One corner of his hard mouth curled. "Now, that's an idea I like." He pushed it into his pocket. "I'll send a check over in the morning."

"You're a nice man, Callaway Steel," she said as they walked toward the door.

He glanced down at her with a wry smile. "That's a new wrinkle. I don't think I've ever been called nice."

"Life is full of new adventures," she told him in her best theatrical voice. "Just think, tomorrow you could be eaten by a shark, or haunted by the ghost of the *Jolly Roger* . . . I wonder if he was?"

He blinked. "Wonder if who was what?"

"If Roger was Jolly." She frowned. "Hmmmm, I'll have to give that one some thought."

"You do that," he murmured, hailing them a cab.

The ride back to the hotel was far too short, and Nikki found herself trying to slow her steps as they went past the desk to the elevator.

"You're dragging, honey," Cal remarked.

"Tired feet," she murmured sheepishly.

"Sorry to see it end, Nicole?" he asked wisely, watching her as they entered the elevator and the door slid shut behind them.

She looked up at him and pain flashed for an instant through her slender body, visible for the blink of an eye in her pale, soft eyes.

"Let's not be serious," she said gently.

He reached out and traced her short, pert nose. "We can't go through life like a couple of clowns.

93

Although you do, don't you?" he added shrewdly. "You use laughter to cover up a lot of hurt."

She looked away toward the neat row of floor buttons on the panel. "And you see too deeply," she countered.

"It wasn't just the flood, was it?" he asked. "Was there a man?"

The elevator door opened in time to spare her an answer, but he wasn't going to let it lie. She knew that by the set of his jaw as he strolled straight and tall beside her toward her room. She'd opened it with her key, but he threw the door back, moved her gently inside the room, and went with her, closing the door firmly behind him.

She stared up at him helplessly. She hadn't meant to invite him in, she hadn't wanted to be so alone with him. But it was going to be impossible to throw him out. And apparently he was determined to get an answer.

"Was there a man, Nikki?" he persisted gently, following her as she went into the room with its neatly made double bed, and onto the small balcony overlooking the bay and the beach.

"Yes," she said with a heavy sigh, leaning on the wrought-iron railing. "It seems like a hundred years ago now, but yes, there was. Ralley was my fiancé. We'd already sent out the wedding invitations and my friends had given me a shower for the household items when Ralley and Leda eloped and got married across the state line." She smiled sadly. "I did so want them to get along. Leda was my best friend, and it was important to me that they liked each other.

Well, they sure did." She laughed, resorting to humor. "They just went a little overboard."

He didn't say anything, but she felt him behind her, felt the warmth of his big body against her back.

"Leda was the one who died in the flood?" he asked after a minute.

She nodded. The wrought iron felt cold and steely under her nervous hands. Being alone with him like this was devastatingly new. Always before there had been people around. But now there were no prying eyes at all.

"Where is the man now?" he asked, moving closer. She felt, with a shock of pleasure, his big hands clasping her waist to bring her back against him.

"He, uh, he lives in a town about fifty miles away from Ashton," she stammered. She felt his warm breath touching her hair, breathed the clean scent of him mingling with the elusive fragrances of his expensive cologne and her light perfume.

His lips touched the side of her neck, running down it to her bare shoulder where the tiny spaghetti straps held up the blouson bodice of the gown. His dark hair was cool where it touched her face, his mouth was warm and slow and its effect was unexpected.

She turned involuntarily to look up at him, the night sounds of surf and song and voices far away drifted nearby like something from a fantasy while she stared into his eyes and found the missing pieces of her own soul.

"You have the most extraordinary eyes," he murmured absently, scowling. "Just when I think I've got the color figured out, they change. They were emerald, now they're aquamarine."

She smiled softly. "Yours don't change. They're very dark." The smile faded. "Sometimes they're haunted."

"I know." He drew in a deep breath. "I carry my ghosts around with me." His hands moved up to cup her face, warming it, caressing it. "Are you a sorceress, Nikki? Can you exorcise them?"

Her nervous fingers reached up to touch, hesitantly, that hard, square jaw, the shadow where the corner of his chiseled mouth began, the imposing line of his nose. He let her touch him, standing quietly, rigidly, as if she were some small animal creeping up to him, and he was doing his best not to frighten it away. Her fingertips found his high cheekbones, his broad forehead, the silky, heavy brows above his deep-set eyes. Then they drew down the rigid muscles of his cheeks and drew across his warm, firm lips with a slow, whispering touch.

"Are you sculpting me?" he whispered softly.

She shook her head. "Just a low-budget safari," she whispered gently. "It's rugged territory, very dangerous."

"It must be, the way you were touching it." His big fingers speared through the hair at the sides of her head and tilted her face up. "Don't ever be nervous about touching me," he murmured, his eyes solemn.

"You don't seem like the kind of man who'd enjoy it," she said. "I mean, being touched by everyone."

"I don't," he admitted. "But, Nikki, I like it very

much when I'm making love to a woman," he whispered at her lips, brushing across hers with his own in a slow, rocking, faintly sensuous motion while his big hands kept her face exactly where he wanted it. "I like being touched, and kissed, and . . . needed. Don't you?"

She felt the slow, nibbling movements of his lips with an ache that sat up and wailed inside her, coaxing her arms to reach up and hold him, her lips to part and invite something rougher, something more satisfying than these maddening little tortures of kisses.

"What do you want?" he whispered in a low, tender tone, his voice sensuous with triumph, with pleasure.

She realized only then that she was reaching up on her tiptoes, trying to capture that warm, elusive mouth, her eyes narrowed to slits, her breath choking her.

"I want you to kiss the breath out of me," she whispered back, the hunger in her voice, her eyes.

"I may do that," he murmured as he wrapped her body up against his, parting her lips with a curt, hungry pressure. "And then I'll put it back again . . ."

She was barely aware of the night sounds all around them, of the music drifting up from the patio, of anything except the feel of Cal's big, hard-muscled body against hers, of the massive arms that were swallowing her.

She'd never felt this kind of hunger before, not with Ralley, not with any other man. It was new and devastating, and she wanted the kiss to go on forever, to never stop. All she wanted from life was the hard, warm hunger of that ardent mouth on her own, and the sweet ache it was kindling in her slender body.

His nose rubbed softly against hers as his mouth lifted to nibble at hers. "It isn't enough, is it?" he whispered gruffly.

"No," she murmured, only half aware of what she was saying. Her fingers tangled in the thick hair at the nape of his broad neck. "Don't stop . . ." she whispered into his mouth as she brought it back down on her own.

"I was hoping you might say that," he murmured sensuously, and all at once he began to deepen the kiss past her shallow experience, to make of it an intimacy beyond any simple joining of two mouths. Nikki clung to him, moaning softly at the unexpected reserves of passion he was drawing from her with his expertise.

"What kind of men are you used to?" he asked in a tone that mingled amusement with impatience. "For God's sake, don't expect me to do it all."

"Then, you'll just have to teach me, Mr. Steel," she whispered at his lips.

He drew back, staring down at her with narrowed eyes that blazed with unsatisfied desire. "Teach you?"

She sighed, watching his face grow even harder. "I hate to ask, but do you have some deep-seated fear of virgins?"

His chin lifted slightly and his hands contracted

98

where they rested on her narrow waist. "You were engaged, you said," he probed.

She nodded. "I was. But to a man I managed very easily to keep at arm's length through the very few weeks before he ran away with my best friend." She sighed softly. "I'm ashamed to say that I wasn't even tempted."

"You're tempted with me," he said. "More than tempted."

She smiled. "Maybe I'm hoping that once I've got over that hurdle, you'll discover that I'm irresistible and you can't live without me."

He released her with a jerky motion and turned away, ramming his hands into his pockets. "Nikki, the world lost all its color when I lost my daughter," he said quietly. "I don't want to get involved again. I don't want children, and I don't want a woman. Not in the way of loving. I've never met a woman I couldn't walk away from. So let's draw back and do some serious thinking before we take that irrevocable step, Nikki." He turned, his eyes turbulent, and stared at her. "I'd hate to see you hurt," he replied softly.

"Thanks so much for all your consideration," she said with evident sarcasm filled with hurt and disappointment. She was deliberately pushing him now, and she realized it, but she was somehow powerless to stop. All that monumental control of his, that cool, arrogant confidence, suddenly irritated her. She was offering herself to him—and he wanted to wait?

"Don't do it, Nikki," he warned quietly.

"Don't do what?" she asked innocently. "Don't

presume to question you? Excuse me, I'm sure you aren't used to people doing that, Mr. God Almighty Steel. You give the orders, don't you?"

He moved toward her like a springing cat, so quickly that she didn't even see him coming until his rough hands caught her upper arms and slammed her into the muscular wall of his body.

"You only want me so long as you can walk away when it's over," she said deliberately, tingling with apprehension and excitement.

"Nikki," he said, and she watched the control snap, watched the dammed-up fury break loose and darken his eyes, tauten his broad face, knit his heavy brows together.

"What the hell kind of game are you playing?" he asked curtly. "What do you want from me? A commitment? I'm sorry, I'm not looking for emotional involvement of any kind. I've had all I can take of it and survive. Marriage is not in my vocabulary anymore." He sighed roughly. "Nikki, I like being with you. I'd like to have an affair with you, even if only for a few days. But that's all I have to offer, take it or leave it."

She didn't look at him. "I suppose all that talk about getting to know each other was part of the approach?" she murmured.

He shifted his gaze uncomfortably. "I didn't want you to feel pressured. But I'm running out of time. I've talked the Jones Restaurant chain's ownership into a merger with my hotels, and the new hotel's off the ground at last. I don't have any reason to stay down here. I've got work to do. I need to go back to Chicago."

"Don't let me stop you, Cal," she said quietly. She still couldn't bring herself to meet his eyes as she refastened the ties he'd loosened on one shoulder.

"Shut up before you push me over the edge," he added in a tight, angry tone.

"And if I do, what happens?" she breathed, her pale green eyes mirroring the excitement that was whirling like a small tornado inside her.

"You know," he ground out, bending. "Damn you, you know . . . !"

Her mouth ached under the rough assault of his, and the hunger of it was a pleasure beyond fathoming. His hands moved, stripping her against every hard, warm curve of his big body from her thighs to her breasts, making her feel every inch of him, the warmth, the power of him.

Her fingers tangled in his dark hair, holding his mouth over hers even though it showed no sign of ever wanting to be free. Her mouth opened, tempted, teased, his, deepening the kiss shyly until he caught her head in his hands and she felt the expert penetration of his mouth in ardent response.

His teeth nipped her lower lip as he drew away, breathing roughly, his eyes dark and narrow. "Do you want me?" he asked curtly. "Because I'm not a boy, and I don't play juvenile games. For me it doesn't end at foreplay anymore. Another minute of this and you'll sleep with me, because we're both human and we want it too much. Now, do I stop while I still can, or do I start stripping you?"

She sobered, like a drunk thrown headfirst into a snowbank. She drew away from him with her eyes lowered, her face paling.

He drew in his breath heavily, like a man who'd been running. Nikki couldn't meet those accusing dark eyes; she didn't try. She felt as nervous as a child taking a shot, and her heart hurt her with its desperate beat.

"You can make me want you, that's very obvious. But so can a dozen other women. I'm not impotent," he said in a voice that made her feel two inches tall.

She folded her arms across her breasts and stared down at the floor. "I'm sorry," she whispered. "It was a stupid thing to do."

"At least we agree about that," he muttered. He lit another cigarette. She hadn't seen him smoke that much in the time they'd known each other. She had a feeling it was something he did when he was angry or upset. He seemed to be both right now.

"I, uh, I think I'll go to bed," she said, feeling acutely embarrassed by her own behavior. She turned to go inside, but he didn't try to stop her, or say a word. He hadn't moved when she closed the door.

She slept fitfully, awaking the next morning with a headache and a sore heart. She didn't know how she was going to face Cal after the spectacle she'd made of herself last night. She still couldn't understand why she'd pushed him that far, unless it had been hurt pride. No, that wasn't all it was, she admitted quietly to herself. It was his refusal to get involved, to commit himself, that had caused her to react that way. She'd wanted more than he was prepared to give, and something inside her had wanted to prove to him that he wasn't immune to her as a woman. She laughed under her breath as she put on white slacks and a matching tank top. No, he wasn't immune to her physically, that was for sure. But what she wanted was the kind of feeling she had for him, the need to be with and comfort and give . . .

She stepped into her low-heeled beach sandals and barely paused to run a brush through her hair before she squared her shoulders and went into the sitting room. She hadn't bothered with makeup, and she didn't care. Cal wouldn't notice. He'd probably send her home this morning, anyway, and she was half hoping he would.

It was nine o'clock, and she'd imagined that he was still in his staff meeting, but when she went out into the sitting room, he called to her from the balcony.

Her heart shifted nervously at his deep voice, but she walked calmly through the sliding door with none of her apprehension showing.

A lavish breakfast was spread out on the wrought-iron table. Cal was buttering a biscuit over a plate dotted with eggs, sausage, ham, and grits.

"I heard you stirring around, so I had breakfast sent up," he said as nonchalantly as if nothing at all had happened last night. "Coffee's in the pot. Help yourself."

She sat down and automatically poured herself a cup, lacing it with cream and a spoonful of sugar. She took a piece of toast, but no eggs or meat, an omission he noticed immediately.

"Not eating won't make it go away," he said shortly. "We're not going to talk about last night, now or ever. It didn't happen. Eat your breakfast and we'll go down to the aquarium and watch the dolphins perform."

"I thought you came down here on business," she murmured quietly.

"I did," he growled. He looked up from his plate. "But right now I think I'd do anything to see the light back in your eyes again."

"I just didn't sleep very well," she said.

He reached across the table and caught her hand in his, swallowing it in a warm, possessive clasp.

"Shall I be blunt?" he asked gently. "Nikki, what you feel is a mild case of infatuation."

She went red from her hairline to her chin, but she met his eyes bravely. "I didn't realize it showed," she said unsteadily.

"I read you very well, Miss Blake," he replied, and his voice was kind. "Nor am I blind. You aren't old enough to build fences around your emotions to hide them. Especially with me. Nikki, you run to me, haven't you ever noticed?" His face clouded. "I'm trying to be as gentle as I can, but I'm hurting, and I can't help it. I want you to understand that it's only the newness of it—I'm simply that, a new experience. Once that edge blunts down, we can be friends. But until it does, you're going to have to keep from putting temptation in my path. I do want you very much, despite everything."

She didn't care about the dolphins, or sight-seeing, or breakfast. Her blank eyes met his.

"If you don't mind terribly," she said in a ghost of her normal voice, "I think I'll go home."

His fork was halfway to his mouth. It never made it. He put it back down and leaned forward on his forearms with a heavy sigh, studying her with unnerving precision.

"I wanted you, too," he said gruffly. "I still do. My God, I ache to my heels every time you walk around the room, but, Nikki . . . damn it!" He shot back the chair and got to his feet, jerking around to grasp the balcony rail and stare down at the crowded beach. "Nikki, you're not ready for that kind of relationship with a man. Not yet, not with me. Men build houses for women like you. They sweat blood to make a decent living, and they look forward to children playing in a fenced-in yard out back somewhere. I've had that. But you haven't. The way you live, where you live, is a world apart from mine. I like my women experienced and unemotional, because an affair is all I want to offer. But the kind of man you'll marry one day isn't going to want that kind of woman, and you know it. He'll want something untouched. A vibrant, happy young woman with a sunny disposition and a body that she'll give to him first, last and always." He stared at his big hands on the railing and sighed. "Honestly, the thought of fathering another child terrifies me," he said. It was in his voice, in those few words: the fear of caring deeply, the fear of losing another child, of losing a woman he loved. He'd chosen the simplest solution.

He wouldn't love again. That way he couldn't be hurt.

She felt the same pain, but for a different reason. He knew she cared for him. That was frankly embarrassing. But at least they were taking care of all the obstacles at once. Perhaps friendship was better than nothing. She'd be with him, she'd get to know him. In time the ache might even be manageable. And in the meantime she could make his loneliness bearable for him, she could erase some of those hard, hurting lines in his face. She could . . . take care of him.

She stood up and moved to join him, watching the blue water wash lazily up on the beach in white foam.

She nudged against him playfully. "I thought we were going to see the dolphins," she murmured. "If you're going to stand here and leer at half-naked women on the beach, I'll go by myself."

He glanced down at her. Miraculously all the hard, deep lines that had been cut into his face began to relax, to give way before a whisper of a grin.

She smiled to herself. It was good to see those melancholy eyes light up. Even if it was only laughter, and not love, that was the cause.

The huge Sea World complex was like a small dose of marine biology, fascinating to Nikki, who'd never been in one before. She went from tank to tank behind thick glass, staring wide-eyed at huge sea turtles, sharks, and a variety of colorful, fascinating creatures, which included dolphins and a baby whale.

"Aren't they beautiful?" she whispered, watching

the sleek, elegant dolphins slice through the water. "But how terrible to keep them confined like this, to deny them the freedom of the ocean."

"Is anything ever free, Nikki—even people?" Cal asked from beside her, his dark eyes narrow and brooding.

"Not completely," she agreed. "But I do hate cages. I hate zoos more than anything in the world."

"Most of the animals that live in them grew up there," he reminded her. "It's the only environment they know. Put them back in the wild and they'd starve, if civilization didn't get them first. Wildlife is dwindling, honey, haven't you noticed? We're paving it out of existence."

"Maybe you're right," she said quietly. "I don't know. I only know how I'd feel if someone locked me up and wouldn't let me go where I pleased. Even if it was in the name of protection."

"Marriage is a kind of prison," he remarked.

"With the wrong person, yes, it must be," she agreed, her mind idly going to Ralley and the unpleasant prospect of the marriage fate had spared her. "But there are happy marriages."

He laughed cynically. "When you put a rich man and a poor woman together, perhaps, so long as she's stacked and—"

Nikki turned on her heel and walked toward the steps that led up to the big tank where the dolphins were scheduled to perform any minute.

"I didn't mean it that way," Cal said tightly, catching her arm as he followed her up the steps.

"You warned me at the beginning that you don't

107

pull your punches," she said quietly. "I'm not that sensitive."

"Then why did you walk away from me?"

She made an odd gesture with her shoulders, shrugging off the slight wound she wasn't going to let him see. "Oh, look," she enthused as they joined the crowd around the tank. Two dolphins leapt into the air in unison to take fish from the trainer's outstretched hands on a high platform.

Nikki's eyes watched them as they went back under the water and swam feverishly side by side, to jump up and rush backward on their tails. Their faces seemed to wear an eternal smile.

"I'm sorry I don't live near the ocean," she murmured under the applause of the other tourists. "I'd love to learn more about dolphins and whales; I've never missed a Jacques Cousteau special yet."

"Intelligent creatures," Cal agreed, following her fascinated gaze to the black and white baby whale opening its huge mouth to receive a fish. "Have you ever heard the recordings of whale songs?"

She nodded, smiling. "Haunting. Beautiful. Like a symphony without music. Did you know that dolphins may be more intelligent than we are?" she added with a grin.

"I'd believe it." He laughed. "They haven't built machines to pollute them out of existence."

"No," she said sadly, "we've done that for them. The days are coming when all animals in the wild will be competing with man for space. I saw a special the other night on the Kalahari, and it was really sobering. So little vegetation, with animals and men

108

competing for it. . . ." She turned her face up to his. "Can it really happen? Can we wind up in a world where the only wild things are kept in cages and on reels of film?"

"Dinosaurs are extinct," he said noncommittally. He shifted his broad shoulders. "I don't know, honey. That's a question for a scientist, not a businessman."

She frowned up at him. "Didn't I read somewhere that you were right in the middle of that wilderness controversy?" she murmured.

He chuckled softly. "I like trees," he told her.

"And contributed to a foundation that's pouring money into finding a way to protect dolphins—a research project on some Caribbean island with protected coves . . . and there was that wildlife preserve . . ."

"I told you I had cats," he muttered, looking faintly embarrassed. "So I like animals, too. So what?"

She only smiled.

They had dinner at a Chinese restaurant, where Nikki ate sweet and sour pork until she felt as if she'd pop. She was lingering over a cup of black coffee when she noticed Cal's eyes following a particularly lovely Oriental waitress. Jealousy surged up in her like bile, and she kept her eyes down so that he wouldn't see it. If she'd been sure of him, if she'd been able to expect anything more than friendship from him, it was an emotion she'd never have known again. Because once he committed himself, Nikki knew he'd never look at any woman but the one to whom he gave his heart.

But he wasn't committed, he was a free agent. And pictures of him with other women invaded her mind, wounding her, hurting her. Of course he wasn't going to live like a monk because they were friends. He wouldn't feel the necessity for those kind of limitations. She shouldn't expect him to. After all, she was equally free, wasn't she? Or was she? Just the thought of being held, being touched, by any other man was frankly repulsive to her.

"Through?" he asked suddenly.

She looked up at him quickly and down again. "Yes. Where to now?"

"Back to the hotel," he said, his eyes idly following that Oriental waitress to the counter. "Wait for me here. I'll get the check." He picked it up and she watched him move toward the counter out of the corner of her eye. The older girl's almond-shaped eyes sparkled as he approached and she smiled; a smile Cal answered. They talked for what seemed a long time, and Nikki felt as if a whip had cut into her flesh by the time he came back and helped her out of her chair.

"Do you have anything planned for this afternoon?" she asked, resolutely concealing the jealousy that was eating her alive. She knew that he'd made a date with the other woman; she knew it as surely as if he'd shouted it.

"No, why?" he asked, frowning curiously.

She went through the door he'd opened, leaving the comfortable air conditioning behind. A wave of hot sea air hit her body like a caress. "I thought I'd spend the afternoon on the beach," she said, stretching with a plastered-on smile.

He walked lazily along beside her the short way back to the hotel. The streets were busy with cars and tourists. Most everything was within walking distance on Bay Street.

"You don't look like you're dying to get on the beach," he murmured, seeing that wildness reflected in her eyes, her face.

She looked up at him innocently. "What do I look like?" she asked.

"I don't know," he said. His dark eyes searched her face. "It's a look I haven't seen in you before. Feel all right?"

"Sure!" she said brightly, and laughed. "I'm having a great time. I'd just like some of that delicious sun. Of course, if you'd planned something . . ."

"In fact, I had," he murmured with a faint smile. "A meeting with two out-of-town oilmen. They're staying on the floor below us, and we've got some problems at one of the rigs that I'd like to discuss. I was going to wait until tomorrow, but this may work out better." He eyed her curiously. "But that isn't going to leave us any time tonight," he added slowly. "I've got to entertain one of the food chain representatives tonight. I may be out all night."

She hadn't dreamed that anything could hurt so much. Food chain representative? Only if an Oriental waitress could be loosely classified that way, she thought with shameful bitterness. But she only shrugged and smiled harshly.

"I wouldn't mind an early night," she lied. "I brought along some material to work on a story with. It will give me just enough time to get it written. I hope you have a great time *entertaining* your *representative*. She sure looked eager enough to me!"

Before he could reply, she took off at a run and didn't stop until she got to her suite of rooms. For the first time, she locked the door between it and the sitting room. Then she threw herself down on her bed and let the tears scald her hot cheeks.

She heard Cal enter the sitting room minutes later. While she sat up, rigid and nervous, she heard other sounds. A door opening and closing. The sound of a shower. Minutes later, the door opened and closed again. Sounds came into the room. A phone being dialed. A muffled, deep voice. Footsteps that paced, coming close to her door for an instant. A hesitation. Then a muffled, harsh sound, followed by footsteps moving away, a door jerked open and being closed angrily. Then silence. A long, stifling silence.

Only then did Nikki begin to breathe again. She wasn't going to worry about mending this wall between them. Not now anyway. She was going to get on her bathing suit, go downstairs, and lie on the beach until the aching stopped. And then she'd think about going home. She could catch a flight back to Atlanta and have Mike meet her. She could always leave a note for Cal. Not that he'd mind, she was sure. It wouldn't bother him that much to lose a *friend.* And no doubt the Oriental woman could console him. . . .

She got up and put on the black and white striped swimsuit she'd brought along, sliding her arms into a white beach robe. Maybe the sun would get her mind off it.

The beach wasn't crowded, probably because most of the tourists were still at lunch, so Nikki picked a place near the water. She laid down on her stomach on the wildly striped beach towel, pausing to unclip the halter of the two-piece suit so that she wouldn't have a line across her back from the suntan. Then she closed her eyes, wiped everything out of her mind, and let the warm sun and watery sound of the surf relax her into a sweet, light sleep.

She awoke to the sound of children laughing nearby. To the murmur of voices. And to a sensation like blistering all over her back.

Her eyes flew open and the sensation got worse by the second. Her back felt stiff, the skin felt as if it had been violently stretched over it until it was to the point of bursting. There was the feel of a giant blister to it, and she knew before she eased the halter clip painfully together that she'd made a terrible mistake in letting herself go to sleep.

The backs of her legs were red, too, but a glance over her shoulder told her belatedly that her back was in much worse shape. With a faint moan, she picked up the towel, slipped into her beach shoes, and went back up to her rooms.

She stripped off the halter and backed up to a full-length mirror in the bathroom, wincing when she saw what she'd accomplished with her impulsiveness.

"Leave it to you," she muttered at her pouting reflection. One side of her face was redder than the other, too, and already she was wondering how she was going to be able to bear anything against her back. She felt faintly nauseated as well. If only she could get some cream on that blistered skin. But how was she going to reach behind her? And worst of all, how was she going to get home? It would be absolute torture to try to sit in an airplane seat—assuming that she could get a dress on over it.

She took the tube of suntan lotion and squeezed out a glob of it, easing it over the portions of her back that she could reach. She winced even at her own light touch. What was she going to do now?

With a muffled sob at her own stupidity she walked back into her bedroom, a towel clutched to her breasts, and lay face down on the quilted coverlet. It looked as if she might have to spend the rest of her life that way.

A few minutes later there was a light tap at the door, followed by Genner's polite voice. "Miss Blake?" he called.

She relaxed. She'd been afraid that it was Cal, but she might have known that he'd never tap lightly at anyone's door. In the mood he'd been in earlier, he was more likely to kick it down.

"Yes, Genner?" she called back, her voice weak.

"May I bring you anything, madam?" he replied. "I'm sorry I wasn't here sooner, but as I explained to Mr. Steel, I was delayed at the post office."

"No, thank you, Genner," she replied. "I . . . I just

thought I'd lie down for a while. I've been on the beach and I'm . . . tired," she added.

"If I can be of assistance, please call," he told her, and his footsteps went away.

Nothing short of new skin on her back would be of any immediate assistance, but she couldn't tell him that. What was she going to do?

She got up and fished a couple of aspirin out of her suitcase. With her susceptibility to medicine they'd knock her out for at least a couple of hours and spare her that much pain. She swallowed them with a glass of water and lay back down on the bed. Minutes later she fell asleep.

A deep voice cut through her restless dream and woke her up, along with a far from gentle touch on her arm.

She gasped, half rising from the bed before she realized that there was nothing protecting her bare torso from Callaway Steel's dark, angry eyes.

With a gasp she dropped back down onto the bed, her face matching color with her back.

"Where did you come from?" she asked drowsily.

"That's a long story," he replied. "What the hell have you done to yourself? Do you realize that you've got a second-degree burn on your back? You little fool, I could beat you!"

"Anywhere but on my back, please," she whispered, with a weak attempt at humor. "I didn't mean to go to sleep in the sun . . ."

He was unscrewing the cap on some cream while she spoke. He noticed her pointed glance at it. "It's an analgesic cream, to take some of the sting out. If you're not better by the morning, you'll see a doctor. Now grit your teeth. This is going to hurt like hell."

She chewed on her lip instead, wincing at even the gentle touch of his big hand as it smoothed the cool cream against the angry burn on her back.

"You crazy idiot," he growled as he smeared it on, taut anger in every hard line of his face. "Why the hell didn't you stay in your room and throw things? There are kinder ways of getting back at a man."

"I wasn't getting back at you," she ground out. "I'm not that petty that I'd do myself in just to get at you," she informed him stiffly. "I just went to sleep, that's all."

"Well, you won't sleep much now," he said with venom in his deep voice.

Tears welled up in her eyes. "And it will serve me right, won't it? Why don't you smooth some vinegar on it . . .?"

"That's enough." His tone was uncompromising, and full of authority. He finished rubbing in the cream. "Genner, bring me a cold, wet cloth."

"Yes, sir," Genner replied from somewhere near the doorway, his pleasant voice concerned.

"What are you going to do, choke me with it?" she asked tearfully.

"Wipe your face," he said quietly. His fingers moved up to smooth the disheveled hair away from her temple. "Want some aspirin?"

The tenderness was her undoing. She couldn't hold back the tears. She told him, tearfully, what

116

time she'd taken the last two, and he calculated when she could have two more. Genner came back with the cloth and went out again, closing the door gently behind him. Cal bathed her hot face with the cloth, his hands tender, his eyes out of sight.

"I'm sorry," she whispered with her eyes closed. "I feel like such a fool. I do want to go home, Cal."

"Like this?" he murmured, and there was amusement in his deep, slow voice. "You'd scandalize the airline."

She tried to smile. "There isn't much to scandalize them with," she managed weakly.

His fingers ran over her soft hair. "There's more than enough," he murmured gently. "You have a lovely body. Exquisite."

She felt the heat in her cheeks, remembering that first surge of consciousness when she'd risen up without thinking and given him a brazenly clear look at her bareness.

"Another first, Nikki?" he whispered gently. "I wasn't disappointed." His fingers moved down to the curve of her shoulder, tracing the inside of it with a touch that made her tremble. "My God, you're perfect."

"Don't . . ." she choked.

"Too intimate?" he asked slowly. "Do you want me to pretend that I closed my eyes? I didn't, Nikki. I couldn't. I wanted to look at you."

Her eyes opened straight into his, and she felt tremors in the very fiber of her soul as she met that dark, quiet gaze.

"How fortunate for you," he said under his breath,

117

"that you're half fried, Miss Blake. Because if you weren't, nothing in this world would save you from me right now."

Her lips parted on a gasp that never got past them. Her heart felt as if it were going to strangle her with its wild beat.

Cal bent, brushing his mouth lightly, tenderly, over her eyes, her small, pert nose. There was a tenderness in the caress that she'd never expected from a man like him.

His fingers traced her soft mouth and he sighed heavily. "My God, you're tangling me up like seaweed, do you realize that?" he growled.

"I'm not trying to," she replied, forcing a smile. "I won't get in your way. I'm sorry about this afternoon. I promise, it won't ever happen again. Okay?"

"It didn't even dawn on me what you meant until I got back to my room," he murmured, ignoring her little speech. "About my meeting. Nicole, that waitress used to work for me in this hotel. She left to marry the man who opened the restaurant. She's just helping out today because one of their regular girls was sick."

She looked thunderstruck. "Oh," she managed.

His face clouded. "And despite the opinion you seem to have of me, I don't seduce the hired help. When I want a woman that badly, I can afford one who knows the score. I don't have to resort to pickups."

She felt ashamed, of her suspicions and her unfounded jealousy. "I'm sorry," she said genuinely. "It was none of my business, and I had no right—"

118

His finger pressed against her lips. "You want me," he said quietly, putting it bluntly. "That gives you the right."

"Cal . . ."

"And I want you," he added, his hard face, his eyes, enforcing every word. His fingers contracted in her hair. "Oh, my God, I want you, Nicole!"

Her lips trembled. She couldn't find the words to answer him.

He drew in a harsh breath and stood up, bending his dark head to light a cigarette. He moved deliberately away from the bed, staring at the carpet.

"I don't know what to say," she murmured miserably.

"There's nothing to say. I've tried every way I know to ward it off, but it's like a damned tidal wave." He made a contemptuous gesture, blowing out a cloud of smoke as he turned to face her. "I don't want marriage," he ground out.

"I'm not asking you for anything," she said, her eyes as soft as the words.

"If we spend much time around each other," he replied, "I'm going to ask you for something. I'm going to ask you for that perfect body that you've never given to a man. And you won't lift a finger to stop me. Will you, Nikki?" he added curtly.

She eased onto her side with a sigh, drawing the towel against her like a security blanket, her eyes sad as they looked up into his. "No," she admitted painfully. "I'd welcome you. You knew that from the beginning. But afterward . . ." Her eyes lowered.

"Twenty-five years of conditioning don't go away easily."

"I realize that."

She shifted, wincing as the sunburned skin protested. "What do you want, then?"

He laughed shortly. "That's a hell of a silly question."

She smiled in spite of herself. Her eyes traced every line of his body, his face, loving the hard, smooth lines of it, almost worshipingly. He scowled at the look.

"Don't worry." She laughed gently. "It's just infatuation. Or desire. Or both. I wouldn't know how to trap you."

"I feel trapped," he said shortly. He finished the cigarette and stubbed it out in an ashtray. "It might be a good idea if we don't see each other for a while. Are you sure you want to cut your vacation short?"

"Yes," she agreed sadly.

He glanced at her. "Your birthday's coming. I'll pick you up in Ashton. I want to take you to New Orleans for some Creole food. As I remember, you told me that was your favorite."

That shocked her, that he should remember something so trivial. But she was learning that he remembered a lot of things that most people dismissed as too trivial. Small, dreadfully important things that endeared him to his staff. To her.

"I'd like that very much."

He smiled halfheartedly. "Are you going to be all right? Genner will bring you a tray."

"That would be nice. Yes, I'll live. I've had burns

120

like this before," she said with a laugh. "The last time I sunbathed, in fact."

He searched her dark green eyes, dark with pain and the pleasure of looking at him. "Are you in love with me?" he asked suddenly, curtly.

She flushed, but she didn't look away. "I'm infatuated," she replied tightly. "Remember? Or maybe I just want an ermine coat and a sports car."

He only smiled. "No, honey, not you. But if you did, you could have them." His eyes narrowed, the amusement left his face. He looked surprised. "You could have almost anything you wanted, with no strings attached. All you'd ever have to do is ask."

"I've got everything I need," she lied. Without him she'd be poor all her life.

"I haven't," he murmured, his eyes sweeping over her body like a tangible caress, dark and hungry and bold. His chest rose and fell heavily, his jaw tautened. He turned away with a quick, graceful movement.

"That business meeting I mentioned was on the level," he said shortly, turning at the doorway. For the first time, she noticed the handsome gray suit he was wearing, the delicately patterned silk tie that complemented it. "There aren't any other women, Nikki. Not now."

His tone implied that there would be, and she managed a faint smile. "Don't work too hard."

"I'll check on you before I turn in. Genner can find me if he has to." His eyes narrowed. "Honey, we can get a doctor . . ."

"Really, I'll be fine," she promised, touched by the very evident concern.

He nodded curtly, even though he didn't seem convinced.

She was half asleep when she heard her bedroom door open. The pain had subsided enough to let her drift off, and she was lying on her side with the sheet around her hips, to keep it away from her back. The cream Cal had smoothed over the burn earlier had taken most of the sting out of it, but the sheet was still abrasive.

She felt rather than saw someone at her side and she opened her eyes drowsily.

"Hello," she murmured sleepily, with a lazy smile as she saw Cal standing there in a black robe.

"Hello, yourself," he replied. His eyes drank their fill of her small, high breasts and the bare curve of her waist before she came fully awake and realized that she was uncovered.

Her fingers reached to jerk up the sheet, but he sat down beside her, stalling the instinctive movement.

"No," he said quietly.

She met his searching gaze levelly, shy with him as she'd never been before, faintly embarrassed at the newness of letting him look at her.

"You have lovely breasts," he said gently, studying them.

Her breath came quickly, unsteadily. The room was dim, and the sound of the sea nearby was like a lullaby. Her own eyes went to Cal's broad chest, clearly visible where the robe had fallen away. It was short, only midthigh, and as robes went, it was of little value as a cover. Almost all of his massive hair-roughened chest was visible, abrasively masculine with its rippling bronzed muscles. His broad thighs were barely covered either, as dark as his chest and sprinkled with curling hair. Nikki had never wanted anything as much as she wanted to touch him. She burned with the hunger, so intent on the sight of him that she missed the narrow appraisal of his eyes.

He reached out and caught her hands, bringing them slowly to the single loop in the belt around his waist.

She looked up, the question, the hesitation, in her wide, pale eyes as time seemed to hang between them.

"You may be disappointed, Little Miss Curiosity," he said with a flicker of humor in his dark eyes. "I'm pushing forty."

While he spoke, he guided her hands, helping them to unfasten the robe. With a single, smooth motion he let it fall to the floor and watched her stunned, absorbed face with patient amusement.

Her eyes fell helplessly to the full, blatant masculinity of his big, powerfully muscled body. She couldn't help staring. It was the first time she'd ever seen a man without clothes at this range, and Cal would have been devastating to an experienced woman. There wasn't an ounce of flab anywhere. He had the conditioned physique of a professional athlete, all darkly tanned flesh and rippling, sensuous muscle under a rugged carpet of curling hair as dark as that on his head.

Her eyes ran over him, then back up to meet his quiet gaze. "I didn't know that a man could be beautiful, until now," she said in a hushed whisper.

His chest rose and fell heavily as he stared at her. "I've been called a lot of things in my time, but never that."

She sat up, her fingers hesitantly, nervously, touching his shoulder, his chest where the dark hair made a wedge against the powerful muscles.

"Do you mind?" she asked breathlessly.

He shook his head, watching her closely. "Did you go this far with him?"

"With Ralley?" she asked. She shook her head with a wan little smile. "Leda came along before he really wanted to that badly. And honestly, I never wanted to at all. I was never curious about him like this. I never ached to touch him . . ." She paused, realizing just how much she was confessing as her eyes levered back up to his.

"I'll let you touch me any way you want to," he said in a deep, husky whisper. His eyes darkened. "But I'm not superhuman, and I do want you like hell. If things get out of hand . . ."

She leaned forward, touching her mouth very gently to his as her hands eased down his massive body and she felt the tremor that rippled under her hands.

"Nikki . . ." he ground out, catching her wandering hands to press them roughly, possessively, against his body and she gasped at the urgency in the motion.

Her eyes opened, looking straight into his, reading the tearing hunger that shadowed them.

"I want to," she whispered shakily. "I want to please you, I want to lie in your arms and feel your body against every inch of me."

"You sweet little fool, you don't even know how to take precautions, do you?" he growled unsteadily, even as he lowered himself onto his back, bringing her down with him. "I hope to God I can keep my head long enough . . . Come here, Nikki. If you want me, show me how much."

She let her body melt down against his, her soft breasts crushing onto his hard, hair-matted chest, gasping at the sweetness of the contact as she ran her hands through the cool, dark hair at his temples.

"Don't let me hurt you," he murmured as his hands traveled gently down her back to her hips and eased them fully over his.

"Cal . . .!" she gasped, stiffening.

His smile was fully male, predatory, his eyes narrowed with calculating amusement. "And this is only the beginning." He laughed softly. "Kiss me, Nikki."

With a soft moan she burrowed her mouth into his, trembling at the feel of his warm, hard fingers brushing gentle patterns on her tender back, her legs, the inside of her thighs, as he deepened the kiss sensually and made of it something erotic beyond words.

He eased her onto her side so that his mouth could smooth the skin of her throat, could take full, aching possession of her taut breasts in the thick silence of the room—a silence broken sporadically by the rasp of skin against skin, by the sharp, shocked little cries that tore out of her throat.

Time seemed to throb into oblivion as he roused her to a point beyond bearing, whispering urgently, coaxing, guiding her until she could feel the tremors wracking her body echoed back by his.

"Now," he whispered roughly, lifting her over him with hands that were at once gentle and urgent. "This is what . . . making love . . . is," he ground out, and as his mouth took hers, she heard a strange, sweet cry echo in her mind while the world spun golden floss as it whirled away into the throbbing darkness. . . .

Dawn was filtering in through the blinds when she opened her eyes and realized where she was. Her head was pillowed on a man's warm shoulder, and she could see the wall across a broad, bronzed chest covered with curling black hair.

Her fingers tangled idly in that carpet above a deep, regular heartbeat and she smiled, shifting her pleasantly aching body with a feline grace.

Her eyes traced the broad masculine face so close to hers, lingering on the imposing nose, the chiseled mouth, the faint shadow of beard on his square jaw. He was good to look at, to lie with. Her cheek gently nuzzled against his shoulder as she drank in the masculine scent of his body that mingled with the remnants of his expensive cologne.

I love you, she thought, looking at him. I love you more than life, and if this is all I can ever have with you, it will be enough. I'll cradle the memory of the night in my mind like a lighted candle, and on lonely nights, I'll take it out and unwrap it and live it all over again. I'll live on loving you until the day I die . . .

His eyes were suddenly open, watching her. "Good morning," she said hesitantly.

His fingers touched her mouth. "Come here and do it properly," he murmured, smiling. She moved, letting her body fit into the now-familiar contours of his. She smiled under his hungry mouth.

"Better?" she teased.

"Much better." He traced the straight line of her nose and smiled into her soft eyes. "How's your back?"

"It doesn't feel blistered anymore," she admitted.

"How about the rest of you?" he murmured.

Her fingers tangled in his thick, dark hair. "The rest of me never felt better," she whispered, leaning forward to brush her mouth against his. "I never dreamed it would be like that," she breathed.

He chuckled deeply. "How did you think it would be?"

She shrugged, nuzzling closer. "I thought it would hurt," she said honestly.

"It depends on the man, my love," he murmured at her ear, "and whether he cares enough about his woman not to hurt her." His fingers tightened at the nape of her neck and he sighed roughly. "My God, you can't imagine how it felt, Nikki," he growled unsteadily. "To hear those wild, sweet little noises you made and to know while I was having you that I was the first man, the only man . . ." His arms hurt suddenly as he drew her breathlessly close. "There's never been a night like that for me."

"You . . . I know you've had women," she murmured.

He drew back and looked down into her misty eyes. "I've never had a virgin, Nikki," he admitted quietly. "So, you see, last night was a first for me, too."

"Did I really please you?" she asked, her eyes telling him how important that was.

"Yes," he replied. His finger traced the long, sweet line of her lips. "Couldn't you tell, you repressed little thing?" he chuckled.

Her mind vaguely recalled a harsh groan, accompanied by the sound of her name being repeated like a litany while he shuddered uncontrollably under her own taut body. Her eyes closed and she nestled against him.

"Yes," she breathed. "Oh, yes, I could tell. I wanted to give you even more . . . ."

He drew her close and his mouth burned against hers in a long, sweet kiss, that left her aching with new sensations, new hungers. She looked up at him, pleading.

"No," he whispered, pressing a finger against her lips, and the smile had gone from his face. "By some miracle I managed to keep my head enough to protect you last night. But I want you even more this morning, and I'm fresh out of magic."

"Would you hate it so much if I got pregnant?" she asked daringly.

His face darkened. He drew away from her and got

out of bed, stretching his huge frame jerkily. "You'd better get some clothes on," he said as he pulled on his robe. "We're flying out about nine this morning."

She sat up in bed, gaping at him. "But you said we'd be here at least—"

He rammed his hands in the pockets of his robe and glanced at her, his eyes hot and possessive on the unconscious nudity of her torso. "I only have so much in the way of self-control," he ground out. "If we stay here another day . . ." he turned away, muttering a curse under his breath. "Don't argue with me."

She watched him until he disappeared into the bathroom. Her green eyes misted with unexpected tears. So it had only been a means to an end. He'd wanted her, so he'd brought her here to make it easier. She closed her eyes and chewed unconsciously on her lower lip as a wave of humiliation washed over her. He wouldn't have forced her, she knew that even now. But she'd given in without a struggle, poor little green fish, and now there was nothing left in her that he wanted.

She dragged herself out of bed and began to get her clothes together. When he came out, she'd have a bath, she told herself, making the thoughts come mechanically. She'd pretend that nothing had happened, she wouldn't ask for what he couldn't give. Tears bled helplessly down her flushed cheeks. What a stupid fool she'd been!

CHAPTER SIX

Nikki showered and changed into a yellow sundress that left most of her back bare, a concession to the blistering that was still uncomfortable. With Cal she tried to pretend that nothing had happened, that things were the same as they had been the day before. But she didn't realize how brittle her voice was, or how false the smile pasted on her lips looked.

"Nikki," he began as they started to get into his small corporate jet, holding her back with a gentle hand, "I want to explain something to you."

"You don't need to," she said with all the bravado she could muster. She even managed a smile. "These things happen. There had to be a first time for me, I'm just glad it was with you."

"You're making it sound cheap," he ground out. His fingers tightened. "It wasn't a one-night stand for me, will you believe that?"

She shifted restlessly. "You told me at the very beginning that you didn't want commitment," she reminded him. "I haven't asked for that, have I?"

He laughed bitterly, studying her wan face. "No, you haven't asked for a damned thing," he agreed curtly. "But I've cut you up pretty badly, haven't I? You look like a ghost of the laughing woman I brought down here."

She shrugged. "I'll get over it."

"Will you really?" His eyes cut into hers. "You're in love with me."

"Infatuation, remember, Mr. Tycoon?" she shot back, her cheeks flaming with sudden color. "I'll outgrow it, you said."

He moved a step closer, and just the warmth of his big body was intimidating, intoxicating. She felt herself beginning to sway toward him, hating her own helpless reaction.

He bent, letting his chiseled mouth stop barely an inch above hers. "Will you . . . outgrow it?" he whispered sensuously. "Come here, Nikki. Kiss me."

With a muffled sob she reached up to drag his mouth down against hers. "Oh, damn you, Cal," she breathed into his demanding mouth as he kissed her roughly, hungrily, crushing her slenderness to him.

He was breathing heavily when he let her go, and his eyes were darkly blazing down at her. "I touch you and it's the Fourth of July," he said unsteadily. "Every sane thought goes out of my head, and I want nothing more from life than the brush of your body against mine in the darkness. What happened last night, I didn't plan. But it wasn't casual and it wasn't

131

cheap." He drew in a deep, steadying breath. "I'm taking you home because I've got meetings I can't cancel, and it's impossible for me to think when you're with me. I'm not walking away from you. I don't even think that's possible anymore."

She stared up at him, dumbfounded, her eyes telling him everything she felt, without a word being spoken.

He traced her trembling mouth with a finger that wasn't quite steady, his broad face somber and dark in the early-morning light. In the gray suit and dark blue tie he looked every inch the conservative businessman. Her fingers rested on his thin white silk shirt, through which the dark shadowy wedge of hair was faintly, sensuously visible. She remembered suddenly how it had felt under her fingers last night while he taught her how to touch him. . . .

"I think I'll wither away from you," she whispered achingly, her eyes searching his. "Like a flower out of the sun."

His fingers caught her by the waist and held her in front of him lightly. "Don't forget, we've got a date. Your birthday."

She smiled halfheartedly. "I'll be ready. But you don't have to—"

"Haven't you learned by now," he murmured deeply, "that I don't waste time doing things that don't please me?"

She studied his dark face. "Do I please you?"

"What a ridiculous question. Get in the plane, you funny woman, before I leave you here."

"Yes, your worship," she murmured, dashing in ahead of him as his dark brows arched threateningly.

Genner sat in the jet while Cal walked Nikki toward the airport office so that she could call Mike to pick her up.

Her steps involuntarily dragged, her eyes glancing off the tall, massive figure beside her. She'd dreaded this moment ever since she'd fallen for Cal, dreaded the parting long before it came. And the hurt wasn't lessened by knowing its inevitability.

He glanced down at her and his face seemed to harden. "It isn't good-bye."

"No, of course not," she agreed with a weak smile.

"Your birthday is a week from Friday, isn't it?" he asked quietly, and she nodded. "I'll be here at five o'clock. Make a note and we'll fly down to New Orleans for dinner. All right?"

Her poor crumpled heart lifted a little and she managed a brighter smile for him. "I'll look forward to it," she said gently.

His eyes dropped to her mouth and lingered on it so intently that it made her lips part in response.

"I wish small towns weren't hotbeds of gossip," he said huskily. "I'd like to break your mouth open under mine and kiss you the way I did last night. I'd like to hold you so close that you could feel how hungry I am for you. And that might shock a few people."

"I'm going to miss you," she said without thinking.

"How do you think I feel, for God's sake?" he

ground out. His dark eyes glittered at her. "If I took you with me, we wouldn't get out of the damned bed for a week. I've got too many irons in the fire to risk it right now, too many people depending on me for their jobs."

Her breath caught in her throat. "Do you want me that much?" she asked.

His chest rose and fell heavily under her fingers. "Until it's almost beyond bearing," he replied solemnly. "But I don't start things I can't finish. I told you how I felt about commitment, didn't I? I haven't lied."

"I know that. I won't ask for something you can't give." She moved closer, her heart in the soft eyes that looked up into his. "Your terms, Cal, all the way."

He scowled. "Don't you want anything?" he asked suddenly.

Her eyebrows arched. "Like what?"

"A car. A fur coat . . ."

She felt a surge of compassion so strong that it almost shook her. Her fingers pressed gently against his warm, hard mouth.

"I'd rather have the memory of last night," she said quietly, "than all the mink coats in the world. Does that answer your question, Mr. Steel?"

He drew her close and held her for a long moment before he spoke.

"I'm glad I made it something you'd want to remember," he said at her ear. All at once he chuckled softly.

"What's so funny?" she prodded.

"The look on your face when I pulled you over me last night," he murmured, drawing back enough to let him see the faint embarrassment that lingered in her face.

She laughed in spite of herself, remembering her own stunned surprise, his faint amusement even in the throes of passion.

"Quite obviously, you weren't aware that it was possible in that position," he whispered. "But it was the only way I could protect your back, you little witch. I'm no lightweight."

She looked into his eyes with a wild excitement making her knees weak as the memory of the long, achingly sweet night pricked her mind. "It was . . . so beautiful," she whispered slowly.

His nostrils flared with a sudden, harsh breath. His fingers tightened on her shoulders. "It wasn't just sex," he said unsteadily. "It was a beginning. Do you love me, Nikki?"

"Yes." Her voice broke on the word, but it was in her eyes, in her face, in her hands that clung helplessly to his waist.

His eyes closed, his jaw tautened for an instant before he suddenly let her go. "Go call your uncle," he said heavily, turning away to light a cigarette. His eyes met hers one last time. "And remember one thing, Nikki. You belong to me now, just as I belong to you. We're not playing games."

She searched his hard face, but not a trace of emotion showed in it. "Cal . . ."

"Keep away from that guy Hall. He had his chance. Now it's mine. So long, Georgia," he added

135

with a last, satisfied appraisal before he turned away and strode back toward the jet. He didn't look back when he climbed into it. Somehow that stuck in Nikki's mind, even when she watched him take off.

CHAPTER SEVEN

Uncle Mike met her at the airport, his deep blue eyes worried, his stocky frame restlessly pacing the concourse. He moved forward the instant he saw her coming toward him and caught her in a bear hug.

"Welcome home, honey," he said with a quick smile. "Are you okay? What happened? Why are you back so soon?"

She laughed nervously and tried not to cry. "Nothing terribly important, Uncle Mike, just a mix-up, that's all." She bit her lip and smiled through a mist. "I'm okay."

He searched her pale eyes and nodded. "We'll talk about it when we get home. Bill Hastings flew me up to meet you. We'll ride back with him in the Cessna."

"Jenny didn't come with you, I don't suppose?" she asked, clutching her single suitcase tightly until he calmly reached down and took it away from her before they started down the concourse.

"The flower club was meeting." He laughed. "Madam President couldn't relinquish her gavel for the trip. But she was as worried as me. Almost," he added dryly.

"I just cut the trip short, that's all."

"So you said." He threw a protective arm across her shoulders and grinned at her. "Welcome home, pilgrim," he repeated. "We missed you."

"I missed you, too," she said wholeheartedly, hugging him back. It would be all right now. Everything would be all right; she was home.

But all the way to Ashton she only listened half-heartedly to the shouted conversation between her uncle and the pilot while her thoughts were back in Nassau with Cal. It seemed like someone else's trip, not her own, now that she was back. Time, which had slowed to a crawl on New Providence, was back on schedule again, and in the airport everyone had seemed to be in a maddening rush. The landscape below the four-place plane looked strange, too, because she'd become accustomed to the sight of palm trees and sandy beaches. Perhaps that would help, the fact that she wouldn't have the island to remind her of Cal with every step she took.

An hour later they landed at the Ashton airport and Mike's big Thunderbird was a welcome sight. Nikki slid in, leaning back contentedly against the black velour upholstery in the white car's interior.

Even in the blazing heat of a Georgia July, it was comforting.

"I need to get an update on the planning committee's recommendations for upgrading this airport," Mike muttered as he cranked the car and turned on the air conditioning. "That might be a good one for you, Nikki," he added as he backed out of the parking spot and headed the car toward the highway.

"I've still got the background material you loaned me to do that last update with," she replied absently. Her eyes were staring blankly out the window at the flat landscape with the thick hardwood trees far on the horizon. Closer was the imposing skyline of Ashton.

Ashton was older than the Civil War, having been founded in 1850. It had flaunted its own proud company, the Ashton Rifles, as part of the Confederate army. Two of Nikki's great-uncles had been members of it, one of whom died at the battle of Cemetery Ridge. The other survived to a ripe old age in Ashton.

A statue of a Confederate soldier stood guard over the town square, while dozens of small businesses huddled in a neat, wide circle around it amid clean air and pretty little trees. The square boasted a large park with benches and sidewalks and masses of flowers donated and cared for by the Ashton Garden Club.

Although Ashton wasn't technically a small town, it wasn't a big city either. It was a nice medium-sized city with a small-town personality, plenty of parking space, good police and fire departments, a daily newspaper, two radio stations, and the weekly newspaper that Mike Wayne's family had founded sixty-five years before. And it was one thing more. It was Nikki's home.

Her eyes lingered on the newspaper office, tucked between the Ashton Pharmacy and the Clinton brothers five and dime store. It was an unimposing little office, with the bulk of its operation tucked away in the back, and Nikki had her own office, next to Mike's. There was one other reporter, "Red" Jones, a typesetter, and an advertising representative.

"Missed it, did you?" Mike asked shrewdly, watching her eyes scan the block for the office.

"I missed a lot of things," she said with a smile. "The refrigerator, mostly."

He chuckled. "For the ice, no doubt."

"And the water. And the soft drinks. And the food." She sighed. "I didn't think I'd ever be cool again. But it was a lovely trip, and I'll be your friend for life if you won't ask me any more about it."

There was a brief pause before he answered. "Okay, honey, if that's how you want it. Now, let's see if we can get enough together to make some sandwiches with before your aunt gets back from her meeting. Then," he added with a grin, "we'll go back to work. Suit you?"

"Oh, yes, it sure does," she said enthusiastically. "Ridiculous as it may sound, I've missed my job, too."

"You love it." He shrugged. "People should enjoy what they do for a living, Nikki. Life is too short to work for the paycheck alone. Money isn't the bottom line."

"To some people, it is," she said sadly.

He glanced at her curiously, but he didn't say anything. Mike Wayne was a veteran reporter, and he read his niece well enough to know that something had upset her pretty badly. But he knew, too, that he'd never be able to pry it out of her. In her own good time, and when she felt ready, she'd talk about it. That was the best part of having Nikki around, that she never tried to hide things from them. She'd been a pitiful little girl, all nervousness and thin limbs and uncertainty. God knew he'd loved her like his own, and Jenny had, too. Maybe they didn't have kids of their own, but Nikki sure felt as if she were. He'd wanted to adopt Nikki years before her parents died. If they'd really wanted her, they had a strange way of showing it. They'd been too wrapped up in each other to care much about Nikki. They never seemed to say more than a few words to her, or to touch her or smile at her.

The Waynes had always gotten along well with Jenny's brother and his wife, but Mike hadn't taken to them privately. He resented their treatment of Nikki, their thoughtlessness. He remembered one Christmas when she was about ten; her parents hadn't even bought her a present. Christmas day, at the family dinner, her father had handed her a five-dollar bill and told her to go get what she wanted. Mike had wanted to get up out of his chair and deck him. But for Jenny's sake he'd bit his tongue almost through and finished his turkey.

Now, holidays and special occasions always got remembered, Mike saw to it. He liked to think he'd made up some of those dark years to that lonely little girl.

The Wayne home was neoclassical in styling, with deep blue shutters around its windows and a fanlight above the front door which tempted the imagination with its intricate, delicate pattern. The grounds were lushly green and shady as dogwoods, pines, and pecan trees mingled around the dark green hedge that separated the circular drive from the house and grounds. Azaleas were in full, glorious bloom, along with the crepe myrtle and wisteria. Jarrat Wayne had built the house the same year he opened the newspaper for operation sixty-five years before. Nikki loved every line of it, and the history it imparted. It was a copy of a much older house Jarrat had seen in the eastern part of the state. His wife had fallen in love with the design, so Jarrat had it copied for her.

"I just had the swimming pool cleaned," Mike told her as he drove the car up to the front walkway and cut off the engine. "Go on in, honey. I'll bring the suitcase."

"Left the door unlocked again, did we?" Nikki teased as she opened the car door and got out.

Mike looked uncomfortable for a minute, sweeping a hand through his silvered black hair. "Well, hell, I only flew to Atlanta and back . . ."

"Someday," she echoed Jenny's eternal argument, "some happy burglar is going to come and carry away every single possession you and Jenny have."

"Every single possession we have wouldn't bring

142

ten dollars," he scoffed. "You know I'm not stupid enough to keep valuables in the house. I don't even buy cheap original paintings anymore."

"How about that antique table that belonged to your great-grandfather's aunt in the West Indies, made of mahogany?" she asked, waiting for him to catch up with her. "And how about the grandfather clock in the hall that Uncle Cecil brought over from Ireland? And how about . . ."

"So I'll start wearing the key to the house around my neck on a chain," he grumbled, gripping the suitcase tightly as he stomped up the steps and threw open the door for her. "Nag, nag, nag . . ."

She laughed delightedly, feeling her old self for the first time since she'd left with Cal. It was good to be home.

"Don't you feel like a swim?" Jenny asked later, when they were relaxing on the patio after a huge supper. "It's a hot night."

Nikki glanced toward her tall, well-endowed aunt who was still dressed in slacks and a tent blouse in a shade of green that matched the eyes she and Nikki shared. Nikki's late father had eyes the same shade.

"I don't see you beating any paths toward a bathing suit," Nikki murmured, laughing at her over a tall glass of sweetened iced tea.

"My figure loses something in the translation." Jenny Wayne laughed. She leaned forward, resting her forearms on her knees, and studied Nikki's slender figure in the casual white sundress. "You look lovely in white, dear, you should wear more of it. By

143

the way, did Mike tell you the news?" she asked, and the tone made Nikki feel apprehensive.

She sat up straighter in the wrought iron chair. "What news?" she asked.

"That's what I thought," she muttered. "Leave poor old Jenny to do the dirty work while he hides in the bathroom."

"What news?" Nikki repeated.

Jenny took a deep breath. "That Ralley's back."

Bad luck seemed to come in bunches, Nikki thought as she sipped her iced tea and tried to look nonchalant. "Is he?"

"Oh, don't play it cool with me," Jenny grumbled. "Who sat up with you all night the day he married Leda and patted you while you cried? Remember me? Long-suffering Aunt Jenny who loves you like a daughter?"

Nikki had to smile at that. She gave her aunt a quick glance. "Okay, long-suffering aunt. I heard you. I just don't know what to say. I thought I loved Ralley, but now I'm almost sure I didn't. I was just in love with love. He's a good reporter, and Mike's lucky to have him back. But as to how I feel about it." She sighed, shrugging. "I don't feel anything. I'm just too numb."

"Not over the flood," Jenny said with a shrewd glance over the troubled pixie face, the downswept thick dark lashes. "So what went on in Nassau?"

Nikki's fingers curled around the frosty, sweating glass. She rocked it gently, listening to the soft, musical tinkle it made. "I met someone," she said.

"You come home looking like a dog whose owner

144

was just run over by a van, with shadows under both eyes and a bitter little smile that says more than you think, and all that boils down to three words. Okay, fair enough. Who, what, where, when, how, and why?"

"I forgot that Mike found you doing rewrites for a daily newspaper." Nikki laughed with a sparkling emerald glance.

"I could have won a Pulitzer," Jenny said haughtily. "I just didn't want to deprive the other staffers of all that opportunity."

"Which means, translated, that after you covered your first wreck you decided the rewrite desk was a nicer memory to take home to supper," Nikki replied. "Right?"

The older woman made a face at her. "Now, if you're through trying to drag red herrings across my feet, how about telling me the truth? If you're ready to, of course, never let it be said that I tried to pry."

"It's nothing, really," she replied quietly, her eyes faraway and sad. "I met a very nice man, we went sight-seeing together and had a great time. But he was really out of my league. I doubt anything'll come of it."

"Nothing!" Jenny threw up her hands. "What do you mean he was out of your league? Was he rich? Famous?"

"Oh, no," Nikki lied. She didn't want anyone to know Cal's identity, much less Mike and Jenny. Love her they did, but Mike wouldn't be above calling up Callaway Steel to give him a piece of his mind if he knew who'd upset the apple of his eye. And Jenny had no secrets at all from Mike; it was one of the reasons their marriage was such a good one.

"He was just an upper-crust man," Nikki said finally, "with an oversized ego."

"Not going to tell me a thing, are you?" Jenny laughed at the expression on Nikki's face. "Don't worry, I won't try to pump you. I know what a sucker you are for tears." She smiled gently. "You really fell for him, didn't you, honey? It happens like that sometimes. I saw Mike, and I knew. Just that fast."

Nikki's pale green eyes clouded. "I wouldn't have believed anyone could care so much, so soon. Oh, Jenny, it hurts so!"

Jenny got up and took the shorter woman in her arms, rocking her, comforting her, as she had years ago when her mother died of the brain tumor and, six months later, when her father ran his truck into the river. She was good at giving comfort to Nikki, she thought sadly; the girl had gone through so much tragedy in her life. Leda's death had been the last straw. She was glad Nikki had found someone to share a few smiles with on that trip. God knows she'd needed it desperately. And if a few tears were the price, they were surely worth it. Nikki's pride would heal, and so would her heart. It was her memories that worried Jenny. She held Nikki closer and stroked her hair.

Ralley Hall was tall and blond and blue-eyed, and Nikki had loved him with all her heart. But when she walked into the office and found him sitting behind the newspaper's editorial desk, she didn't feel anything at all except a friendly warmth and sympathy.

"Hello, Ralley," she said gently, shaking his hand while Mike Wayne watched nervously. "How are you?"

He shrugged. "Coping," he replied with a faint smile. "I sold the house and moved back here," he added. "The memories were too much. Even the job reminded me of her." His face contorted, and she saw the sadness in it for an instant before he erased it. He'd looked like that at the funeral.

"You'll enjoy being back," she assured him, trying to keep her memories out of the way. "Mike might even let you do the update on the airport, if you bribe him with a fifth of bourbon."

Ralley jumped right in, staring over Nikki's shoulder at the older man. "Really?" he asked with arched eyebrows.

"Depends on the brand," Mike said with a grin.

Ralley mentioned a well-known one, and Mike nodded. "It's yours. Just as well, Nikki doesn't know the fuselage from the altimeter."

"I do so!" she said indignantly. She tossed back her short, dark hair with a haughty hand. "I'll have you know I could have been the poor woman's Wright brothers with just a little more training."

"Remember that airplane model I got you for Christmas two years ago?" Mike asked her. "The one you put the wings on upside down?"

Her face flushed. "They weren't marked."

"Most people know what they look like."

"I got the propeller in the right place," she reminded him. "One out of two isn't bad."

"Weren't you going to interview the mayor on that new water system we're getting federal funds to build?" he asked her.

"Right!" she said, backing out of the office. "You bet. I'm on my way. Good to have you back, Ralley."

Ralley smiled, and it was genuine. "It's good to be back," he said, and meant it. It was in his whole look.

"Pictures," Mike reminded her.

She made a face. "I'll forget to put film in the camera again," she protested.

"I already loaded it. Bye!"

She shook her head as she walked toward her own office. "Oh, the perils of being a journalist . . ." she mumbled.

The next few days went by in a rush. Nikki forced herself to keep busy, not to think about the past at all. She and Ralley were still a little distant with each other, but she was beginning to understand Mike's reason for bringing the reporter back. Ralley was a good editorial writer, one of the best. He got his facts straight, and he wasn't afraid to state them, despite the flak. He wouldn't pass the buck to Mike either. If an irate reader called, Ralley talked to him, soothed him, explained his point of view, and listened to the reader's. He'd matured a lot in the past year, ever since Leda's death. But what Nikki had once felt for him was gone forever.

On the other hand, Ralley was noticing Nikki in a way he hadn't before, even when they were engaged. She'd just been someone to go around with back then, pretty and cute and sparkling. But Nikki had changed, too, she was much more of a woman now, and Ralley found himself regretting his impulsive elopement with Leda. Not that he hadn't cared for Leda; he had. But no one knew how strained the marriage had become in the past few months. Leda and he had been perfect together physically. She'd given him something that Nikki had never tried to give. Where Nikki was chaste and reserved and unresponsive, Leda had been a veritable volcano. She'd captivated him, and he'd let himself be led to the altar. But once the first few weeks of marriage had dampened those high-burning fires, he'd begun to notice things about Leda that he hadn't noticed before the marriage. She was lazy. She didn't like housework, she hated to cook, she wanted to be with him constantly. He couldn't even escape her in the evenings; she followed him around like a puppy. In desperation he'd suggested that she might enjoy a job of her own, but she'd refused flatly to go to work. She had a husband to do that. All she needed to do was look beautiful and make sure his clothes went to the cleaners once a week.

Probably they'd have wound up in divorce court eventually, but Ralley wasn't sharing that tidbit with anyone. Let them think it was the perfect marriage; it would be better for all concerned, especially for him. If Nikki felt sorry for him, he might have a chance of winning her back. This new Nikki was exciting and he sensed a new maturity in her. And since there was obviously no other man in her life, she'd probably never gotten over him. He'd smiled secretively at the thought. How sweet of her to pine over him. Perhaps he wouldn't have to try too hard after all.

It should have gotten better. She should have been able to put Cal in the back of her mind and finally blot him out of it entirely. But each day the wanting was worse, the ache was worse, until she wound up awake until two and three o'clock every morning, pacing, pacing, like a caged little animal.

Her mind fed on him, on bits and pieces of memory that she threaded and sewed into a silken veil to clothe the raw wound inside her that being without him had caused. She went to work mechanically, she did interviews, she wrote stories, she took pictures, she helped make up the paper, she stripped in corrections and wrote headlines. But nothing she did gave her any pleasure. She grew melancholy and pale, and even Ralley began to notice how dull her emerald eyes had become, how her steps dragged. She barely ate at all anymore, drinking cup after cup of black coffee and walking the floor at night.

Cal was probably out with a new woman every night, she told herself, and cried just at the thought of another woman holding him, touching him, caressing him with her eyes as Nikki had, loving him . . .

She was literally mourning him, and nothing eased the pain, nothing lessened the gnawing hunger for him.

Late on Friday night she was reluctantly watching

a police drama with Mike when Jenny went to answer the phone.

"Nikki, it's for you," Jenny called, and there was a note in her voice that puzzled the younger woman.

Nikki lifted the receiver and said, "Hello," bracing herself to fend off Ralley one more time.

"Hello, yourself," came a deep, unmistakable voice from the other end of the line.

She felt a tingle of excitement the length of her body and had to sit down because her knees buckled. Easy, girl, she told herself, easy.

"How are you?" she asked politely.

"How the hell do you think I am?" he growled. "You don't sound so good yourself."

She cleared her throat. "I've been working hard," she told him.

There was a muffled curse. "Look, meet me at the Ashton airport in an hour."

It was like an electric shock, lifting her from the chair. "Do what!" she burst out.

"You heard me. One hour." And the line went dead.

She sat there looking at the receiver with the same expression a fisherman would have on his face if he threw in his line and pulled out a chicken dinner.

"Well, was it him?" Jenny and Mike chorused, watching her from the doorway of the living room.

She nodded.

"Is he coming here?" Jenny asked, poised to grab a broom and a mop and head for the stove to cook.

"I think so. He said to meet him at the airport in an hour."

151

"He's coming." Jenny took off like a shot.

"I'll put some ice in the cooler for drinks," Mike murmured, following her.

Nikki clutched the receiver against her, cradling it, rocking it, while she finally let the tears loose.

She was sitting at the airport in Mike's T-bird fifteen minutes before Cal was due, with the doors locked and the CB unit on as Mike had made her promise, since the airfield was deserted. The airport manager's family lived in the mobile home just beside the apron, and their lights were still on. Mike had probably called them, too, Nikki thought with a smile. He and Jenny were like a couple of mother hens with a chick over her. It was good to have people care about you, even if they did carry it to extremes. Nikki didn't know what her life would have been like if it hadn't been for them.

A droning sound caught her attention. She straightened her white shirtwaist dress and primped in the rearview mirror under the dome light, making sure her face looked its best with the hint of soft pink lipstick, her dark hair curled toward her face in a soft style that she hoped suited her. Her fingers trembled as she nudged it into place, her heart was shaking her in its fury.

A small jet dropped down onto the runway with precision point landing, coming easily to a stop to turn and taxi onto the apron. On the side was painted STEEL AVIATION.

Nikki was already standing on the pavement, her

eyes straining to see the door opening in the spill of the nearby streetlights.

A tall, big man in a pale suit came quickly out of it and stepped decisively toward her. Before he made another move, she was running to him, her arms open, her eyes blurring him as tears veiled them.

"Cal!" she cried.

His arms opened as she reached them. He caught her, lifted her, crushed her against him, finding her mouth with his in one smooth, rough motion to take it as if it had belonged to him since time immemorial. She clung, giving him back the kiss, holding him, sobbing wildly as the world melted away in her mind and there was only the feel of his arms and his mouth, the scent of him, the reality of him. It was like coming home after a long, lonely journey.

"Am I hurting you?" he whispered huskily against her mouth. "Nikki, am I hurting?"

"No." She kissed him back hungrily. "Oh, no! Cal, I've missed you . . ."

His mouth broke against hers again and again, tasting, touching, demanding. There had been a slight chill in the air, but she was warm now, wrapped up so closely against his massive frame, safe and protected in the circle of his big arms.

She gave him everything that she had in the way of response, holding back nothing. Her body seemed to burn everywhere it touched him, aching, clinging to the powerful lines of his.

"I'll always belong to you," she whispered breathlessly. "Whether you want me or not. . . ."

"I want you," he said in a deep, rough tone.

She leaned her forehead against his chin, fighting to catch her breath. Her body felt molten, liquid, and she clung to him for support.

His breath came with as much difficulty as hers. He stood quietly, holding her until his hard, heavy pulse calmed, until the faint tremor went out of his powerful arms.

"My aunt's in the kitchen, cooking," she whispered. "Can you stay?"

"Only the night," he murmured quietly. "I'm due in Panama City by six o'clock tomorrow night for an early meeting with some of my staff. I just stopped by to see you."

"Oh, I see." She took a small, hurting breath.

"No, I don't think you do." He smiled.

"Would your pilot like to come along?" she asked, glancing back toward the plane.

He eyed her with faint amusement. "I founded Steel Aviation and you're asking who flew me?"

Her eyes went from the plane back to him. "I thought it was oil."

"Oil came first. When I had the money, I went into hotels and aviation." He smiled at her confusion. "I like airplanes, don't you?"

"Oh, yes, but I don't think I could fly a jet. Even a baby jet."

"I'll teach you." He slid an arm around her shoulders and pulled her close against his side. "Oh, God, you feel good to me," he murmured, brushing his mouth against her temple. "I didn't know how lonely I was until I left you. I'm sorry this has to be such a short visit. But I'll be back again in a week—on

154

your birthday. Don't you forget, I'll be at your house at five P.M. sharp to pick you up. Okay?"

She smiled up at him, her face brightening. "Okay." He held the car door open for her, but when she sat behind the wheel, he slid in and pushed her aside with his bulk. "Move over," he said. "Nobody drives me except me. Not even you."

"Well, I like that!" she said indignantly, giving him just enough room to fit under the steering wheel. He slid the seat back to allow his long legs room enough to fit under the wheel and lifted an eyebrow at her.

"Woman's libber," he accused.

"Male chauvinist pig," she came right back.

He laughed as he pulled the car away from the airport. "You color the world for me," he murmured. "I think I'd forgotten how to laugh, how to play, until you came along."

She lowered her eyes, the memory of that night between them, but she smiled. "I'm glad you think so."

"Well, direct me, unless you want to drive around in circles all night!" he teased, and she turned her attention to getting them home.

When they arrived at her door, she got out of the car in a fog, allowing herself to be escorted up the steps and into the house.

"Don't they ever lock this door?" Cal asked when he discovered that he didn't need the key Nikki had handed him.

She laughed softly. "Uncle Mike forgets. Someone

constantly nags him about it, but I think it's gotten to the revenge stage now."

"I like this architecture," he murmured, studying the entrance hall and the staircase. "Neoclassical, isn't it?"

"Yes, and there's quite a story behind it; remind me to tell you someday." She took off her light jacket and tossed it on the back of the sofa in the living room. Mike and Jenny were nowhere in sight.

Cal took off his suit coat and loosened his tie. "God, it's hot here," he murmured.

"We used to have air conditioning," she said apologetically, rising to turn on the big window fan, "but Mike got a horrible allergy to it and we had to take it out. Fortunately it doesn't stay this hot year round, and he isn't allergic to heat. Don't you want to change into something . . ."

"More comfortable?" he suggested with a grin.

She flushed, glancing away from his wicked gaze. "I thought that suit might be hot."

"It is. Care to help me take it off?"

She opened her mouth to speak, but he was having such fun at her expense, it seemed a shame to spoil it.

She walked over to him and began to unfasten, slowly, the buttons on his silky vest. Her eyebrows levered up at the expression on his broad, dark face. "You asked for help. I'm only trying to be hospitable."

His big chest rose and fell roughly under a skirl of deep, pleased laughter. "Imp," he murmured, reaching down to jerk her body against him. "Delightful,

156

little pixie." The smile vanished, and his eyes were lonely, still. "My God, I've been lonely, Nicole!"

It was like coming back to life after being buried. All the weight of depression lifted, floated up, soared away, and her eyes burned on his face like pencils making sketches. He was so good to look at, to touch, to be held by. And she'd missed him unbearably. She recognized that loneliness in his eyes, because it was a mirror of her own.

"Cal, I've missed you, too," she whispered fervently. She bit her bottom lip, searching his face, his eyes, hungrily. All at once her arms went up to him and he lifted her, crushed her, against his big, warm body. "Kiss me . . ." she pleaded, her voice breaking, splintering as his dark head bent and his mouth took hers.

He was rough this time, as if the waiting had worn him, tried his patience, as if he'd never expected to see her again in this life.

"I missed you," he repeated against her eager, soft mouth, his voice deep, husky, his arms hurting as they crushed her into his huge frame. "You took the sunlight with you, the music . . . God, Nicole, I've been lonely before, but never like this."

She went up on tiptoe to give him back the kiss, all sensation, all woman. She felt him tremble in her arms with a sense of wonder at her own power.

"Come home with me," he groaned. "It's a huge town house, there's more than enough room . . ."

"And be what, Cal?" she asked quietly, searching his eyes.

"My woman," he said.

157

She shook her head with a sad, hurting smile. "There's another name for a woman who lets herself be kept by a man. I don't want it." She drew away from him. "Besides," she said, staring out the dark window, "I have my own life here, a job I enjoy, roots . . . We did agree not to make any commitments, didn't we?"

He was silent for a long moment before he spoke. "I guess we did," he said curtly. His eyes were accusing as they met hers. "I knew you were going to be trouble the minute I laid eyes on you," he added.

She smiled despite the heartache that was eating at her. The temptation to give in was great. But not as great as her own self-respect, and she couldn't sacrifice that to become an expensive plaything. She went back to him, reaching up to kiss him again. "Let's live one day at a time, okay?" she asked softly.

He grimaced. "I suppose we'll have to. Flying visits, like this, phone calls . . ." His mouth crushed down against hers. "Never mind, just kiss me and ease the ache a little."

Mike and Jenny came in together a few minutes later, exchanging smug glances when they found Cal and Nikki deep in conversation in the living room. Nikki looked up, only just realizing that they must have gone for a drive to give her some privacy with Cal, and she flushed as she met Jenny's eyes.

She made the introductions, noticing the easy way Cal was with her aunt and uncle, as if he'd known them for years. He and Mike spent the rest of the evening discussing stocks, bonds, politics, and aviation, while Jenny and Nikki murmured and listened.

"How about some more coffee?" Jenny asked finally. "I've got a pie in the refrigerator . . ."

"None for me, thanks," Cal said, rising. "It's been a long day for me, and if you don't mind an unsociable visitor, I think I'll have an early night. I'll have to fly out tomorrow afternoon for a meeting in Panama City."

"Mike will show you which room," Jenny said with a smile. "We're glad you could stay, and I'm sure Nikki is," she added.

Cal smiled at Nikki, his eyes possessive. "I hope so," he murmured. "Good night, honey."

"Good night, Cal," she murmured.

"Oh, you've got tomorrow off," Mike called over his shoulder. "You can't leave Mr. Steel to sit around the house alone."

"Cal," their guest corrected. "I'm only Mr. Steel to my enemies." And, with a grin, he left the room.

"Now," Jenny began when they heard a door close upstairs, "do tell me all about that nice small businessman you met in Nassau. Remember, the one with the oversized ego. . . ."

"I should have his ego," Mike moaned as he rejoined them, dropping down into his big armchair by the dark window. "A corporate giant, in my home."

"Reach for your pad, and I'll strangle you," Nikki said mutinously. She stood over her uncle with hard eyes. "He's a guest, not a walking news story. Okay?"

Mike grimaced. "Nikki . . ."

"Promise me, Uncle Mike," she wheedled, "or I'll

159

tell Aunt Jenny about that blond stewardess . . ." she added in a whisper.

His jaw dropped. "That was completely innocent!" he whispered back.

"It won't be when I get through with it. Well?" she asked.

His face pouted, his blue eyes met hers accusingly. "I may never forgive you," he reminded her.

"It won't be the first time, either," she said gaily.

"I do occasionally read financial magazines," Mike said. "Callaway Steel is something of a legend among tycoons, you know."

"He is something, period." Jenny sighed. "Oh, if I were a few years younger, and Mike wasn't so sexy . . ."

"He's a good bit older than you are, Nikki," Mike said gently.

She sighed. "I know. But it doesn't matter. We're only friends, Mike." Her voice was more wistful than she knew.

"He looks like he'd be dynamite," Jenny murmured.

"He is." Nikki sighed, walking right into the trap.

"And don't hand me that 'just friends' routine," Jenny added with a wink. "He didn't come all this way just to say hello. By the way," she added, patting Nikki's cheek as they went into the hall ahead of Mike, "your lipstick's smeared."

Nikki wouldn't have touched that line with a shotgun. "Good night," she called as she raced up the stairs.

* * *

160

"Is it always this quiet?" Cal asked lazily as he and Nikki lounged by the private lake under a towering oak tree on the grassy lawn the next morning.

"Most of the time," she agreed. She was lying on her stomach in a bright yellow sundress, watching Cal, who was stretched out on his back wearing slacks and an unbuttoned brown plaid shirt. His thick, dark hair was mussed and fell into unruly patterns on his broad forehead. It made him look younger, but those hard lines in his face were still very much present.

She tickled his imposing nose with a blade of grass, laughing when he caught her wrist and pulled her over so that she was propped up on his broad, partially bared chest.

"I like you in yellow," he murmured, opening his eyes to study the peasant-blouse styling of the dress. "It suits your personality."

"Mushy?" she asked with arched brows.

He frowned. "How did you get that?"

"Well, you said it reminded you of my personality, and butter is yellow but mushy. . . ."

He chuckled softly. "Your mind would fascinate a research scientist."

"Ummmm," she murmured. She only half heard him; she'd just discovered a faint dimple in his chin, and her fingers were tracing it.

"What I meant," he murmured back, linking his hands behind her, "was that you're sunny."

She smiled. "Thank you."

His dark eyes searched hers. "Life hasn't been

kind to you," he said gently. "Neither have I, in a lot of ways. It's hard for me to trust people, Nikki."

"I know. It's hard for me, and I'm not rich," she said gently. Her soft eyes searched his. "Did you really think I was after you because of who you were that first day?"

"Yes," he admitted. He looked up through the leafy, sun-patterned branches of the oak. "It's an old ploy with women to pretend indifference to get a man's attention. You caught mine that first day, with that bathing suit tantalizingly visible under that next-to-nothing coverup. You have gorgeous legs, Miss Blake."

She laughed disbelievingly. "But you were horrible . . .!"

"Self-defense," he said softly. "I wanted you on sight. I thought if I made you mad enough to stay away, I'd forget about you. Then you started running, and that old hunting instinct took over, in spite of my misgivings. When I found out you were a reporter, it all blew up in my mind."

"You don't trust reporters, I gather."

He met her eyes. "Nikki, I've been harassed to death by the press." His dark face seemed to stiffen. "You've heard about what happened, I gather? That my daughter was killed in an automobile accident and that my . . . wife died a few months later? The media had a field day with it. And every time I read another story speculating on Penny's death, I had to relive it all again."

"Penny was your wife, wasn't she?" she asked quietly.

He nodded. "A beautiful woman. Blond, blue-eyed, utterly gorgeous. But it was only skin deep. She hated me, she hated the idea of a child, she hated anything that took her away from her mirror and her admirers. She had two lovers the first year we were married." His jaw tautened. "I didn't love her. The marriage was more of a merger than anything else. But after Genene was born, I told her if I ever caught her with another man, if there was a breath of scandal, I'd cut her off without a cent and she'd never see Genene again. It was very effective, in one sense. She gave up men. But she substituted drugs for them."

"Didn't she care for you?" she asked, incredulous.

"No, honey. She gave what little affection she was capable of to Genene. There wasn't anything left over for anyone else. The night of the accident I was away at a conference. Penny decided to leave Genene with her grandmother so that she could go on to a party. She was high when she left the house." He took a slow breath. "She never made it. I'll never forget how I felt when the call came. It was just as well that it took me four hours to get home. I wanted to ring Penny's neck."

She could imagine how it must have been for him. Under those layers of reserve he seemed to be a deeply emotional man; the kind who'd love completely, not holding anything back.

He flexed his broad shoulders, shifting. She started to get up, but his grip was formidable. "Penny sobered up pretty quickly after that, but she couldn't live with the guilt, not without some anesthetic. It kept taking more and more, and every time I'd send her off to be dried out, she'd start again. It reached the point where I couldn't even reason with her anymore. One night she took a few pills too many. It was already too late when the maid found her."

She searched his dark eyes. "And ever since, you've been asking yourself, 'What if . . .?'" she murmured.

He looked faintly shocked. "You don't miss much, do you?"

"I know how it is," she replied. "My mother died of a brain tumor, there was no help to be had. But my father and I had just had an argument the night he was killed." She dropped her eyes to the pattern of his shirt. "You know how kids can be. He and my mother were devoted to each other. They never had time for me. After she died, it was even worse. I'd gotten the lead in our school play, and it was the night we were putting it on. Dad refused to go, or even to drive me there. I ranted and raved about it until he slapped me." Her eyes closed on the memory. "I didn't say another word, and neither did he. He walked out the door. Thirty minutes later Uncle Mike came to get me." She sighed. "They said he was driving too fast for conditions. But it was suicide. He didn't want to live without Mother."

Cal's big arms swallowed her, drawing her gently down against him, comforting her, soothing her. His fingers worked in her hair in a slow, rhythmic motion, and she could feel the steady, strong beat of his heart against her breasts.

"What was your daughter like?" she asked softly.

His chest rose and fell slowly against her. "Like

me, strangely enough," he murmured. The words came hesitantly, and Nikki sensed that he hadn't talked about it to anyone until now. Perhaps there wasn't anyone he could talk to, unless it was his mother.

"Dark?" she prompted.

"Dark hair, dark eyes. Tall, for her age. All legs and big eyes." He laughed gently. "She liked to climb trees, which horrified her mother. Ladies weren't supposed to do that, but Genene was a tomboy through and through. I bought her a horse and Penny went up like a rocket, but Genene was a born rider. We'd get up early every morning and go riding before I went to the office." He laughed shortly. "Once I walked out of a board meeting in the middle of a proxy fight to take Genene to a birthday party."

"What happened?" she asked.

"I won." He chuckled. "The deciding votes came from a stockholder who was delighted at the sight of a man willing to give up an empire for a birthday party."

She laughed with him. "But you didn't do it for that reason, I don't imagine."

"No, I didn't. Hell, anytime they think I'm not showing enough profit, they can throw me out with my blessing. But that hasn't happened, and it won't happen." His arms tightened. "I had cake and ice cream with the kids. Genene won a prize for pinning the tail on the donkey. You'd think she won the Nobel prize, the way she beamed." He drew in a short breath. "A week later she was dead. I've thanked God on my knees ever since that I didn't tell

165

her I was too busy to take her to that birthday party." He sighed heavily. "If only I'd been at home . . ."

She drew away far enough to look down into his dark, sad eyes. She laid a finger across his hard, chiseled mouth. "You couldn't have prevented it if you'd been standing across the street," she said gently. "Any more than I could have taken my father's foot off the accelerator, or stopped my mother from getting a brain tumor. . . . Cal, I don't pretend to know all the answers. But God sees farther down the road than we do; perhaps he's protecting people from something we can't foresee by drawing them to him." She smiled quietly. "I like to think of it that way, at least."

Her fingers traced his mouth, her eyes lingered on the chiseled curve of it. Impulsively, she leaned down and brushed her lips over it, feeling a delicious shiver of sensation at the light contact.

"Do you mind?" she whispered achingly.

His chest rose and fell quickly, heavily. "I need it as much as you do, Nikki," he replied in a deep, taut whisper. "I need you. . . ."

His arms brought her down to him, and he made a harsh, muffled sound as her mouth opened over his. The action tightened the arms around her bruisingly as he whipped her across his big body and onto her back in the lush, green grass with the weight of his broad chest crushing her down into it.

His mouth was hungry, rough, slow, and achingly thorough on the petal softness of hers. She felt the nip of his teeth against the full lower lip before his

166

tongue drew a sensuous path over it, past it, in a sudden, sharp intimacy that dragged a moan from her throat.

Her arms slid under his, her hands easing past the hem of his cotton shirt to caress his warm, bronzed back over the hard, silky muscles. Her fingers dug into it, tested its strength, as his mouth became more demanding on hers.

He levered away from her all at once, his eyes dark with unsatisfied desire, his jaw as taut as the muscles in his powerful arms as they supported him.

"No more, Nikki," he said in a husky voice. "We're getting in over our heads."

Her fingers lingered on the damp flesh of his back, her eyes mirroring the conflict that was going on inside her. She thought ahead involuntarily, to the end of the day when she'd watch him fly away and she'd stand on the runway and feel an emptiness like death inside. The thought took the light out of her eyes, the smile from her face. How was she going to manage life without Cal in it? Would the memories be enough?

He took a long draw from the cigarette he'd just lit and turned, his face more composed, his eyes calm if a little dark.

"It's just as well that we aren't still in Nassau," he said with a wry smile.

She made a face at him. "I used to think I had loads of willpower until you came along," she admitted shyly. "With Ralley, I was always reserved, very cool. He used to complain about it."

He didn't like that reference; she read the distaste in his dark eyes. "Ralley?" he asked.

"Ralley Hall. He, uh, came back to work for Uncle Mike this week," she added reluctantly.

Cal's dark head lifted sharply. "How convenient."

She hated the ice in that deep voice. She scrambled to her feet with worried eyes. "Cal, it was over long before the flood," she told him. "I gave him up the day he and Leda married, and I never wanted him back. I still don't."

His taut features relaxed a little. He took a long draw from the cigarette and studied its orange tip.

"Did you ever let him touch you the way I have?" he asked suddenly, staring straight across into her eyes.

"No, Cal," she replied. "Not ever."

He moved forward, dropping a careless big arm across her shoulders in a gesture that was more comradely than loverlike. "I'd like to see where you work," he said as they walked back toward the house.

Which meant, she thought nervously, that he wanted to see Ralley. At least he was that interested in her. But was it only a physical jealousy, or was he beginning to care?

She wasn't going to sacrifice her hard-won peace of mind to that kind of reflection, she decided firmly.

"Suppose we drive by the office then?" she asked pleasantly.

He nodded. "That suits me."

Now, if only the police would arrest someone important so that Ralley would have to leave the office to cover the story. . . .

She should have expected to find her former fiancé in his office, poring over the week's columns to check them for errors and make sure they'd fit the space he'd allowed.

He stood up when Nikki walked in with Cal at her side. Cal had exchanged his casual clothes for a dark blue blazer with an open-necked white silk shirt and white trousers. He looked like a fashion plate and Nikki wanted more than anything to show him off. He was so good to look at.

But if she thought so, Ralley didn't. His blue eyes turned cold when they met Cal's, and that dislike was reflected in the older man's dark, piercing eyes.

"How do you do?" Ralley asked as if he couldn't have cared less, when Nikki introduced them.

He held out his hand, but Cal hesitated a few seconds before he took it, treating it like dead meat.

"This is the editorial office," Nikki said, jumping in. "Ralley is our news editor. He does most of the editorial writing and substitutes for me at city and county council meetings when I'm tied up elsewhere. He edits column copy, too."

"Nikki's never needs editing," Ralley murmured, giving Nikki his most ardent look. He came around the desk to slide an arm affectionately around her shoulders, grinning when she stiffened in shock. "She's a super little writer," he added, "and I tell her so twice a day, don't I, darling?"

Cal didn't say a word; the expression on his broad

face didn't change. But something in the gaze he pinned to Ralley's face made the younger man remove his arm and back away.

"I'll show you around," Ralley volunteered. "Thursdays aren't too hectic, except for phone calls protesting what people read when the paper comes out on Wednesdays. The really bad day is Tuesday, when we go to press. That's when we all scream and tear our hair out and curse the telephone."

"It rings like mad all day long," Nikki added with a tight smile. Cal was as remote now as if he'd been shot to the moon. She couldn't understand Ralley's brazen move any more than she could understand Cal's reaction to it. Surely he didn't believe there was anything between her and Ralley? Surely Ralley didn't think she still cared. . . .!

"This is where the type comes from," Ralley told Cal, indicating a computer with a screen and a keyboard like a typewriter, with two extra narrow keyboards on either side. "It's a computerized system, brand new, just like the big-city papers have. Reporters mostly set their own copy, but we have Billie to set the filler stuff and the legals," he added with a wink at the petite blonde behind the computer.

"Is the newspaper printed here?" Cal asked quietly.

"No," Nikki told him. "We have to carry it all the way to Mount Hebron, thirty miles away. At that, it's still less expensive than buying the setup we'd need to do it here. We do all the makeup and paste-up, get our own ads and make them up—everything, in fact, but the actual printing. Mike drives the paper

170

down there Wednesday morning and we get it back by that afternoon. Then we all rush to the back, run the papers through the mailing plate machine to put the names on the local papers, bag the single wraps, and get it in the mail. It's in the boxes Thursday morning."

"And nobody comes by the office on Thursday and Friday, because they don't want to bother us while we're working on the paper," the redheaded reporter, aptly named Red Jones, piped in, pausing to introduce himself and short, dark Jerry Clinton to the newcomer.

"Nobody realizes that we do that on Monday and Tuesday." Clinton grinned. "It's a deep, dark secret."

"These two handle the police beat and the advertising, respectively," Nikki said. "We're all interchangeable, of course, and we all do makeup and paste-up."

"And Jenny keeps the books," Mike broke in, joining them. "Came to see if I was working, huh?" he teased Nikki.

Cal arched his eyebrows at the neat, orderly operation. "I expected to find a desk buried under reams of paper and old journalism books and yellowed back issues stacked on shelves. I'm impressed."

"You should have seen the place when my father was alive." Mike chuckled. "He used to inspect the office once a week wearing white gloves. God help the staff if he found dust. Care for some coffee? We have our own snack bar in the back."

"No, thanks," Cal replied before Nikki could open her mouth. "I've got some phone calls to make."

"See you at the house, then," Mike murmured, sensing undercurrents.

"Nice to have met you," Cal told the rest of the staff, his eyes stopping short of Ralley.

They echoed the polite remark. Ralley, seeing opportunity slamming at his door, moved forward and tugged a lock of Nikki's hair in an old, affectionate intimacy.

"See you later," he said, keeping his tone uniform with the gesture. "Take care of her, Mr. Steel," he added with a curt smile.

"Good-bye, Ralley," Nikki said, her glowing eyes promising retribution at the earliest opportunity. "Thanks for all your help."

Ralley ignored the sarcasm. No way was he going to let that big-shot outsider swipe his girl. He'd seen Nikki first, and he wasn't giving her up. He didn't plan to let her slip through his fingers this time. He'd been a fool to let her go, but Leda's charms had blinded him. He was older now, and wiser, and he wasn't going to hand Nikki over to some expensive stranger. She couldn't be serious about that big man, anyway; God knew he was years older than she was. Mike had mentioned something about him being a tycoon, but Ralley was skeptical. After all the guy could have been pretending. But even if he did have all that money, it wouldn't take the place of love. Nikki still loved him, he told himself smugly. All he had to do was prove it to her. He walked back into his office whistling.

* * *

"Are you going to ignore me for the rest of the day?" Nikki asked as she and Cal sat down alone to a small lunch.

Cal glanced at her, dark-eyed and unapproachable, over his coffee cup. He'd been pleasant enough since that visit to the office, but it was all on the surface.

Cal was just as remote as he'd been on the drive home, and she wondered if a sledgehammer would dent him.

"I won't be here for the rest of the day," he said quietly.

"You're leaving?" she asked, her eyes wincing, her disappointment almost a physical ache.

"I'm a businessman. I've got too many irons in the fire to stay here." He finished his coffee.

She'd noticed that he'd changed into a beige suit, with a matching tie, that he was dressed for travel, not recreation. But she hadn't wanted to believe it. Now she had to.

She wasn't sure, but she thought she knew the reason he was leaving. If she was wrong, it was going to be horribly embarrassing. But if she wasn't, she'd have been a fool to keep quiet.

She laid her napkin beside her plate and drew in a steadying breath. "I am not having an affair with Ralley Hall," she said quietly. "I am not involved with him in any way. I can't explain why he put on that show for you, but that's all it was. A show."

"That isn't what he told me," he replied curtly, and his eyes were cold.

173

She frowned slightly. "But he didn't talk to you . . ."

He put down his own napkin and stood up. "I called him while you were fixing lunch." He shot back the cuff of his shirt and checked his watch. "I won't be able to wait until your aunt gets back from her shopping trip. Tell her I appreciate her hospitality very much. I've already thanked your uncle, and phoned for a cab to take me to the airport."

She caught his arm hesitantly. "Cal, what did he tell you?" she asked, fearing the worst.

He looked down at her with the cruelest expression she'd ever seen. "Come on, honey, don't give me that. No wonder your conscience bothered you about your friend. Did she know you were seeing her husband behind her back?"

Her heart fell over in her chest. Ralley had told him that! How could he, how *could* he!

"It's not true!" she burst out, horrified. "Cal, you've got to believe me!"

He removed her hand from his jacket, gently but firmly. "I don't know what to believe anymore." His dark eyes searched her face narrowly. "You wanted him before he married your friend. You loved him, you said. Well, nothing's changed except that she's dead and he's free."

Nothing? she wanted to say. Everything had changed. And it hadn't been love she'd felt for Ralley, she knew that now for certain. It hadn't torn her heart out by its roots when Ralley had left, it had only hurt her pride. What she was feeling now made that remembered agony less painful than a pinch.

Losing Cal was a little like dying. She didn't know how she was going to breathe when he was gone.

"Why won't you believe me?" she asked sadly. "Is it because you don't want to? Does it give you an excuse to keep from getting involved? You didn't have to worry about that, I wasn't going to try to trap you." She turned away and sat back down at the table. "I learned a long time ago that you can't make people want to be with you, any more than you can force them to love you." Her fingers reached for the half-full cup of coffee in front of her; she swallowed it down quickly and got to her feet, dabbing at her mouth with her napkin. "It was nice to see you again. If you'll excuse me, I'm already late for work."

She didn't look at him as she went out the door, hiding the tears that threatened to spill over onto her pale cheeks. Neither of them said a word about work, although they both knew Mike had told her she didn't have to come in.

As she drove with determined calmness down the driveway, she didn't even look back. She was hurting too much.

Ralley looked up sharply when she walked into his office and slammed the door behind her, shutting them off from the rest of the staff.

"Why?" she asked venomously. Her eyes were still red from the tears, her voice shook with controlled fury.

He knew what she meant. He got up from behind the desk with a conciliatory smile on his handsome face. "Now, honey, don't get all up in the air. He's an old guy, much too old for you."

"Is that what you told him?" she asked.

"Sure. It was the truth," he said defensively. He approached her, but she backed away, her eyes openly hating him.

"What else did you tell him?" she persisted.

He stopped, leaning his back against the desk, not so confident now. "That you loved me," he said hesitantly. "You do, don't you? You always did, even when I married Leda, I knew it. Nikki, I missed you," he said softly, leaning toward her. "Leda was a lovely girl, a sweet girl. But she wasn't you. If I'd just kept my head and waited, it would have blown over. We'd have got married. . . ."

"And made each other miserable for the rest of our lives," she finished for him, certainty in her pale green eyes as they cut into his. "I was infatuated with you. God help me, I'd probably have gone through with the wedding if you hadn't eloped with Leda. But it's all over, Ralley. You're beating a dead horse. It's too late."

His lower lip protruded. "You're just upset," he said soothingly. "But you'll get over it," he added smugly, smiling at her before he went back to sit at his desk. "When you're calmer, we'll talk some more. You haven't got over me yet, Nikki. I'll show you."

"The only thing I want to see is your back walking away," she grumbled.

"Don't pretend you cared about the big man," he said sarcastically. "Maybe he had a fat wallet, but he was years too old for you. Besides," he added shrewdly, "what would a man like that want with a small-town girl like you? Maybe you were a novelty for a while, but you wouldn't fit into his kind of society and you know it."

She did, and it cut like a double-sharpened knife. She turned around and walked out of the office without bothering to reply. There was nothing she could say, anyway.

For the next week Ralley did everything but sit on her doorstep and play a flute to get her attention. He followed her to the local drugstore at lunch and sat with her until she started going home in desperation. She couldn't seem to move without bumping into him. When she heard the phone ring at night, she knew before she answered that it was Ralley with another invitation. He'd invited her out every night since Cal left, and she'd turned him down every time. She was too raw inside at what he'd done to want his company again, ever. But Ralley was persistent. It was what made him a good reporter. He never gave up.

"You're looking pale," Jenny remarked gently one day over a ham sandwich. She'd served it on the patio with the remark that Nikki needed some fresh air.

"It's from running," she replied lightly. "Ralley thinks he can get me back if he's persistent enough."

Jenny watched her closely while she bit into her sandwich. "Can he?" she murmured.

Nikki shook her head. She stared into her cup of

black coffee, leaving all but one bite of the sandwich on her plate untouched. "I told him it was over, but he wouldn't believe me."

"What, exactly, did he tell Mr. Steel?" Jenny asked after a minute. "You haven't talked about it, and I haven't asked. But it's going to explode inside you if you don't let it out."

"I don't know all of it," she admitted bitterly. "He told him he was too old for me, and that I'd been seeing Ralley while Leda was alive, too, apparently."

Jenny ruffled indignantly. "Why didn't you tell Mike? He'd have thrown him out the door!"

"That's why," came the dry reply. "Ralley's a good reporter, Jenny. He only wants me because I'm not available, that was why he chased me the first time, years ago." She laughed softly. "Funny, I didn't like him at first. Now I don't like him at all." Her face fell. "Cal wouldn't believe me when I told him Ralley was lying."

"Then maybe he cared more than you knew," Jenny murmured. "He'll be back, honey. Just calm down."

"He won't be back." Nikki got to her feet. "Thanks for the sandwich. I've got to cover an emergency services meeting at city hall, then I'll be at the office."

Jenny only nodded, watching her niece walk stiffly away.

But being calmer didn't help to sort anything out. As the days went by, she found herself under siege again by Ralley, who seemed more determined than ever to get her back. She didn't flatter herself that it was love causing his acquisitive spurts. Ralley simply had a dogged determination to obtain anything that resisted him. It made him a good reporter—but a nagging suitor.

"I'm afraid to sit in the living room," she wailed to Jenny as they sat by the pool. "I expect to find him leering at me from behind the potted plant!"

"Won't give up, huh?" her aunt teased.

Nikki leaned forward, propping her chin on her hands. "Never. I'm so tired of dodging him. I seem to have done little else since I came back from Nassau." She laughed mirthlessly. "Funny, isn't it? There was a time, when he was sneaking around to see Leda, that I'd have given anything to make him care. And now it doesn't matter at all."

"Because now you're in love with someone else," came the wise reply.

She nodded. "Desperately," she admitted with a wan smile. "The question is, where do I go from here? I'm not kidding myself that Cal will ever want to marry me. He and I move in different circles, and he's told me himself that the thought of having another child terrifies him. He doesn't even want a commitment. He told me so." Her eyes clouded. "He hasn't even called me."

"You said he was going to be up to his ears in meetings," Jenny reminded her.

She laughed bitterly. "And that shows you the place I occupy in his thoughts, doesn't it? I'm not even as important as a board meeting. Do you know he walked out of a board meeting in the middle of a proxy fight to take his daughter to a birthday party?" she asked her aunt.

"It sounds like something he'd do," Jenny replied, smiling. "And remember, he came quite a long way to spend a day with you."

"But that was before . . ." She turned away. "It doesn't matter."

"I don't want to raise your hopes too high, my darling," the older woman said gently. "But he had the look of a man deeply in love."

Nikki sighed. "But, then, so did Ralley . . . once," she reminded Jenny with a faint smile. And before the subject had the chance to come around again, she got Jenny off on recipes.

Friday finally came. Her birthday, and Nikki had been nervous all day, wondering if Cal would remember his promise to take her to New Orleans. Mike had given her the afternoon off, swearing that she was of no damn use in the office except for wearing ruts in his floor. Ralley had overheard the conversation, and Nikki had the oddest feeling that he was up to something. But of course, he wouldn't have the opportunity to disrupt her plans again. She'd see to that.

Jenny had gone to visit friends, and Mike had to drive to Atlanta for a conference on an editing workshop he was helping with, so Nikki had the house to herself. In a way that was worse than having it full of people. She dressed in a two-piece white knit suit that showed her tan off to advantage, and white strappy sandals. Then she paced the floor and bit her lip, eyeing the clock every few minutes and wondering.

Cal had said that they belonged to each other. But wasn't that pretty much what a man said when he'd been with a woman for the first time? He hadn't wanted the relationship to get that involved, he'd said so often enough. But he'd given in to his own hunger, and perhaps it was guilt that had caused his remarks. He'd been the first, and he knew it, and he was sometimes pretty old-fashioned in his outlook. He might be permissive, but he still harbored feelings of responsibility, and it wasn't inconceivable that he could be that way about Nikki.

She stared at the clock again. It was only ten minutes until five. If he was coming, he'd be there on time. Cal was nothing if not punctual.

Only ten more minutes and she'd see him again. Maybe only five more minutes. Her heart quivered madly in her taut body. It seemed like years since she'd seen him, held him. Centuries! It didn't matter if he didn't love her, as long as she could be with him for even a few minutes, see him, touch him. Oh, God, she loved him so!

A sound caught her attention and she froze in the middle of the room. It was a car coming up the driveway. It was Cal!

She ran for the door as the car pulled up at the steps and she peered blindly through the curtains, trying to see through the layers of gauzy fabric. . . .

She gave up and opened the door just as a tall man

bounded up the steps. Her heart sank. It was only Ralley.

"What are you doing here!" she burst out.

"I've got to pick up something for Mike—if you don't mind," he added sarcastically.

"Oh, all right, but will you please hurry?" she ground out, peering around him toward the deserted driveway.

He went into the study and ruffled through some papers on the desk. His narrowed eyes studied her quickly.

"Uh, it sure is hot out there," he murmured, tossing her a brief glance. "Do you think I could have a small glass of wine—just to take off the top layer of heat?"

"Ralley . . .!"

"I know Mike keeps a bottle of port chilled." He grinned. "Come on, Nikki, have pity on a poor, hot reporter."

"All right, but just one glass," she muttered, running for the kitchen. "I'm going out."

He murmured something, but she didn't stay around long enough to hear it.

Her ears strained for the sound of a car as she poured him a glass of the chilled port from the refrigerator and raced back to the study to hand it to him.

"Ummm," he murmured, sipping it. "That's delicious. Thanks, Nikki."

She was literally wringing her hands. Why didn't he go? The sound of a car caught her attention.

"It's Cal!" she burst out. But as she moved, so did

Ralley, and seconds later, the port was all down the front of her white knit suit.

"Oh, Nikki, I'm so sorry!" he burst out, grabbing a handkerchief from his pocket. "Here . . ."

"That won't do, you idiot, I've got to change!" She couldn't let Cal see her like this! "Ralley, tell Cal I'll be right down!" she told him, and dashed up the stairs.

The minute she was out of sight, Ralley began to take off his clothes. By the time the doorbell rang, he was down to his briefs. He walked calmly to the door, with the wineglass still in his hand, ruffling his hair in the process. He wiped the smile off his lips just as he jerked the door open.

Cal, dressed in dark evening clothes with a shirt that probably cost more than Ralley's entire wardrobe, seemed to implode at the sight of the younger man.

"Where's Nikki?" he asked in a deep, softly dangerous tone.

"Upstairs, waiting for me, of course," Ralley drawled, lifting the empty glass. "She'll be sorry she missed you. . . ."

"Cal!"

They both turned as Nikki gaped helplessly at the tableau below, dressed in nothing but her slip, the dark stain of the wine just faintly visible where it had seeped through. Her face contorted in something like agony. What Cal obviously believed was in his taut expression and she saw immediately that it was going to be useless to plead her case. Ralley smiled inso-

183

lently, and Nikki wanted to strangle him with her bare hands.

"Hello, darling, look who's here." Ralley laughed.

Cal's huge fists clenched at his side. He didn't say a word to Nikki, but his dark eyes spoke volumes. He turned to Ralley and with a move so quick that Nikki missed it, he threw a shattering punch at the younger man. Ralley didn't have time to dodge it. It caught him square on the jaw and sent him sprawling sideways on the polished wood floor.

Cal's blazing eyes went from the fallen, groaning man on the floor to Nikki, frozen on the staircase.

"Excuse me for breaking up the party," he said in a voice that dripped ice water. "I thought we had a date, but obviously I was mistaken."

He spared Ralley a final, contemptuous glance before he opened the door and stormed out.

Tears bled down Nikki's pale cheeks. She couldn't remember a time in her life when she'd hurt as much.

Ralley dragged himself to his feet, gingerly touching his jaw. "He's got a punch like a mule," he groaned.

Nikki only stared at him, hurting like she'd never hurt before.

Belatedly he looked up and saw her face. He stood there, watching her with eyes in which comprehension began to shine. "You really love *him,* don't you?" he asked quietly.

She didn't even answer the question. "Please get dressed and go away," she said in a ghost of her normal voice. "You can't imagine how silly you look."

She turned and went back into her bedroom, closing the door firmly behind her.

There was a faint knock at the door.

"Nikki . . ." Ralley called through it, his voice sad, faintly embarrassed. "Nikki, he wrote telling you he was coming. I . . . I intercepted the note at the office. I'm sorry."

But she didn't answer him. She was crying too hard.

CHAPTER EIGHT

Nikki went downstairs an hour later, when she'd had a bath she didn't need and put on a beige pant suit and blotted her eyes for the tenth time. She'd cried until her eyes were raw. But all the tears in the river wouldn't bring Cal back, and she knew it.

Ralley had gone home, and it was beginning to get dark outside. Nikki poured herself a glass of wine and dumped it down her throat. She still felt miserable, so she refilled the glass and drank it down. Damn Ralley—when she got herself together enough, she was going to kill him. On second thought there must be something worse than that she could do to him. Perhaps she could write a false exposé on the police chief and publish it under his by-line. She remembered the size and temper of the public official and smiled halfheartedly. Ralley would be turned into chili powder. Unfortunately so would Mike, who would be blamed for it. With a sigh she refilled the glass once more and sat down on the sofa.

It was just as well, she told herself. Cal lived in a different world. She'd never have been able to cope. Her eyes teared again and the hot, bright dots rolled pitifully down her cheeks.

Her mind went homing back to Nassau, to that unexpected night with Cal. All over again she could feel his hands, so tender, so wary of hurting her, his mouth blazing on her bare skin while he whispered words that still could make her blush.

She got up, almost tripping over the rug, and walked the floor, sipping at the red wine. She'd never see him again. She'd grow old and spend her miserable life trying to make do with memories. And it just wasn't going to be enough. All the memories on earth wouldn't amount to one minute with Cal.

"I always seem to love the wrong men," she grumbled, tossing off the rest of the wine. She stared into the empty glass, frowning slightly. Where had it gone so fast? Perhaps she'd spilled part of it. She remembered Ralley pouring the glass of wine down the front of her white outfit and her lips pouted wildly. Without thinking she flung the empty glass at the fireplace and watched it splinter. Good enough for it. It wouldn't stay full, anyway.

Bells sounded in her ears. She blinked. Surely she wasn't that drunk? She shook her head and listened. There it was again, that funny chiming. . . . Of course, she thought with an off-center smile, it was the doorbell. Mike must have forgotten his key. Or it could be Ralley again. . . .

She made her way toward the front door. If it was Ralley, she was going to kill him. She was debating on methods when she opened the door, and found a ghost standing there.

Cal was still wearing his evening clothes, but his tie was untied and the top buttons of his expensive ruffled white silk shirt were undone. He looked tired, angry, and exasperated, all at once.

Her lower lip trembled. "Oh, Cal," she whispered brokenly. Without thinking she held out her arms, wondering vaguely if he'd push her away.

He moved forward like a conquering army, jerking her against his big body to lift her while his mouth crushed down on hers. She felt the tremor shake him even while he deepened the kiss, his tongue penetrating, his breath sighing raggedly against her cheek as his arms contracted painfully around her.

Tears rolled helplessly down her cheeks when he finally paused long enough to take a breath. Her fingers caressed his broad, darkly tanned face, trembling.

"It wasn't true, it wasn't . . ." she whispered unsteadily.

"I know." He kissed her again, letting her body slide down his until her feet touched the floor. "I'm so sorry, darling," he whispered roughly. "God, I want you . . .!"

Her arms linked around his neck and they swayed together wildly, so lost in each other that they were aware of nothing else. Her thighs trembled against the hard muscles of his, and she thought wildly that if she died right now, it would be enough that she'd held him, kissed him, one last time.

"I love you," she whispered into his devouring mouth.

He trembled convulsively at the words, drawing back to look into her misty, wide eyes. "I love you, Nikki, for always," he whispered back, his voice shaky, his eyes punctuating the incredible statement.

"But . . . you said . . ." she faltered.

He smiled faintly. "I know. But that was before I tried to function without you." He drew in a steadying breath, taking time to reach behind him and close the door.

"You were so angry," she whispered, searching his dark, soft eyes, "I was afraid you were gone for good. Ralley intercepted your note—I never even saw it— and he staged that whole scene. He spilled wine on me and when I went upstairs to change . . ."

He smoothed the hair back from her tearful face. "Hush, darling, it's all right, I'm here now." He bent and kissed the tears from her eyes. "I remembered when I got to the airport that there was a wine stain on your slip and an empty glass in his hands. And along with that, I remembered something else."

"What?" she asked, smiling wetly.

He brushed his mouth across hers. "That you loved me," he said simply. "So I came back."

Her lips trembled, her eyes widened. "You could have gone away, and I'd never have seen you again. . . ."

"That's not likely." He lifted her, carrying her

easily into the living room, to sit down in Mike's big armchair with Nikki in his lap.

She nuzzled her face into his warm throat. "I wanted to kill Ralley. . . ."

He chuckled softly. "Hush, it's all over. I'm here, and I love you."

"That's the second time you've said it," she whispered.

His big arms tightened. "If I keep saying it, perhaps you'll begin to believe it." He eased her head back on his shoulder so that he could see her face. "Didn't you hear what I told you before I left the last time? That we belonged to each other?"

"I thought it was just because you were the first . . ."

He sighed deeply. His fingers toyed with the hair at her ear. "Nikki, all the time I was spouting those clichés about not wanting commitment, I was making plans. Hundreds of them, and they all included you. Vacations in France, buying a house outside Chicago, buying furniture . . . none of which I could picture without you. And something else, something more . . ." He tilted her eyes up to his. "Nikki, the next time we make love, I'm not going to hold back. I want a child with you."

That was the final surrender, she thought wildly, that was total commitment.

Her fingers traced the lines of his hard, chiseled mouth. "I'd like very much . . . to give you a child," she whispered softly. "Very, very much."

"Then suppose you put this on," he murmured,

drawing a box out of his pocket, "and we'll go somewhere and discuss it."

She turned the black velvet box in her hands curiously before she opened it over a blaze of emeralds. Her breath stopped as the two rings filled her gaze. An engagement ring, and a wedding band ringed around with emeralds and diamonds. She looked up at him.

"Cal . . .?"

"I'm good in bed," he reminded her. "And I don't have many bad habits."

She laughed through her tears as she buried her face against him. "Oh, I love you so!"

He laughed gently. "When do Mike and Jenny get home?" he asked.

She drew back and sat up. "Oh, not for three or four hours at least," she murmured, peeking up at him through her lashes.

Without another word he got up, lifting her with him, rings and all, and started up the staircase. She clung to him, her eyes full of emeralds and babies and the long, sweet years ahead.